Michael Underwood
THE UNINVITED CORPSE

M
MACMILLAN
LONDON

C305787999

Copyright © Michael Underwood, 1987

CB

First published in 1987 by
MACMILLAN LONDON LIMITED
4 Little Essex Street London WC2R 3LF
and Basingstoke

Associated companies in Auckland, Delhi, Dublin, Gaborone, Hamburg, Harare, Hong Kong, Johannesburg, Kuala Lumpur, Lagos, Manzini, Melbourne, Mexico City, Nairobi, New York, Singapore and Tokyo

British Library Cataloguing in Publication Data

Underwood, Michael
   The uninvited corpse.
   Rn: John Michael Evelyn   I. Title
   823'.914[F]   PR6055.V3

   ISBN 0-333-43324-6

Typeset in Baskerville by Bookworm Typesetting, Manchester
Printed and bound by Anchor Brendon Ltd, Essex

CHAPTER 1

'GOODBYE, DEAR,' Mrs Henderson shouted through the car window above the engine noise.

Her sister-in-law responded with a perfunctory wave and disappeared inside the house before Olive Henderson had time to engage a gear and move off.

As an energetic, and often unappreciated, doer of good works she was impervious to the reactions of those around her. Once she perceived where her Christian duty lay, it took more than a force-ten gale to deflect her from her purpose. She had been a widow for twenty-five years, and the less charitably disposed of her acquaintances had been known to suggest that her husband, seeing what was in store for him, had departed hastily to the next world after a mere four years of married life.

It was a fulfilment of Christian duty that had taken her to visit her widowed sister-in-law in Oxford. The two women had never got on, but Mrs Henderson went regularly twice a year for a four- or five-day stay. She regarded her sister-in-law as a spoilt, complaining woman with too much money, and in return was seen as bossy and insensitive, particularly where her sister-in-law's feelings were concerned.

It was with a feeling of relief, but of duty satisfactorily performed, that she now headed home in her small car. It would be another six months before the occasion had to be repeated.

Mrs Henderson lived at Mongton-on-Sea where she had a flat on the sixth floor of a block not far from the sea-front. Her neighbours on the same floor were a Mrs Fox, a Mr Welling and a Mr Gray. Mr Gray had much the largest flat, with an enclosed sun-terrace which ran its whole length. Mrs

Henderson had singled him out as a target for her Christian duty almost as soon as he moved in, which had been about two years ago. Recently there had been slight friction with the arrival of his latest live-in housekeeper. Mrs Henderson had made it clear, however, that she brooked no nonsense from anyone's employees. The woman (her name was Janet Berry) was obviously jealous and quite unsuited for the post. She had been hired by Mr Gray's solicitor, Rosa Epton, and Mrs Henderson proposed telling Rosa of her unsuitability at the first opporunity.

It was around four o'clock when she drove down the slope to the underground garage and parked her car in its usual place. After a quick tidy-up she would go across the landing and invite herself in for a cup of tea with Mr Gray. She would tell him about her impossible sister-in-law and satisfy herself that Janet Berry hadn't been neglecting him while she had been away. Though it never occurred to her that Mr Gray didn't appreciate her visits, she had on occasions found him giving her what she could only describe as secretly amused glances, such as would have disconcerted a more sensitive person. It was almost as if he were mocking her for her inability to enter his private world. Not being given to introspection, however, she never bothered to wonder about these occasional arcane looks.

The only sound of life on the sixth floor when the lift decanted her came from Estelle Fox's flat. Mrs Fox, now in her seventies, had been a not particularly successful profes-sional singer who liked to pretend she had been a great diva in her heyday. She was singing an aria from *Turandot*, which Mrs Henderson had heard all too often through their dividing wall. She was singing fortissimo, and the sixth-floor landing rang with sound. Mrs Henderson had on more than one occasion asked if it was necessary to sing so loudly, but to no avail.

She let herself into her flat and closed the door to shut out the worst of the noise. She soon unpacked her small suitcase, had a good wash, and was ready to go and ring Mr Gray's bell. Mrs Fox was still singing as she recrossed the landing.

Normally, Janet Berry would open the door immediately, but it now remained firmly closed. Mrs Henderson rang the

6

bell a second time and for longer, but without response. She concluded that the housekeeper had slipped out for a few minutes and that Mr Gray, who was slightly deaf anyway, was having a prolonged siesta.

Lifting the letter-box flap she peered through. All she could see was the deserted kitchen and the half-open door of the housekeeper's bedroom. There was no sound of life.

After giving the bell a third ring and still getting no answer, she returned to her own flat. After pondering the situation she decided there was little she could do for the moment except go on trying. During the next couple of hours she alternated phone calls with trips across the landing.

By now she was sure something must be wrong and she must find out what. A first step was to discover whether her neighbours knew anything. With luck Mr Welling might be able to provide a clue. That is, if he was in. He owned a number of clubs in the town and was often out from around midday until the small hours of the morning. Mrs Henderson was unsure what went on at his clubs, and thought she would probably disapprove if she knew, though she had always found him a courteous neighbour. He had never given her cause for complaint, though she was aware that he sometimes entertained young ladies at his flat.

As she had surmised, however, she got no answer at his door and was left with no alternative but to tackle Mrs Fox. She was certainly at home and still in full voice. Mrs Henderson pressed her bell and kept her finger on the button until Isolde broke off her declamation of love to the dead Tristan and came to the door.

Even if she lacked the voice, she had the figure of a dramatic soprano. She had a massive bosom and long tresses of faded golden hair and, surprisingly in view of her age, a youthful peaches-and-cream complexion.

She now stood before Mrs Henderson in one of her numerous caftans with her tiny slippered feet peeping out beneath the hem.

'I was singing,' she said unnecessarily. 'I thought you were away.'

'I came back this afternoon. I've been trying to get in touch with Mr Gray, but can't obtain any answer. Do you know

7

anything? Has he been taken ill?'

Mrs Fox shook her head vaguely. 'Not as far as I know.'

'When did you last see him?'

'You know I don't remember things like that. It was probably some time last week. I'm not on friendly terms with him the way you are. Not since he was so rude to me.'

'What about Mrs Berry?'

'I don't believe I've seen her going in and out, either. She may be away.'

'I'm sure I'd have been told if that were the case. She never mentioned going away when I went in to say goodbye to Mr Gray before I left last Thursday.'

'Then, I can't help you. She may have had to go off suddenly and arranged for Mr Gray to go into a nursing home for a few days. As a matter of fact, I wasn't well myself over the weekend, and today's the first day I've been singing again. I still have to take great care of my voice, you know. I'm hoping next month to record excerpts from some of my most famous roles.'

Mrs Henderson shot her a suspicious glance, but was met with a distinctly challenging expression.

'So what do you propose to do?' Mrs Fox now said. 'About Mr Gray, I mean.'

'If I've been unable to get any answer from his flat by tomorrow morning, I shall notify the police.'

'Isn't that over-reacting?'

'Certainly not,' Mrs Henderson retorted sharply. 'He could be lying dead inside.' She paused. 'I never did trust that Janet Berry.'

'Surely you're not suggesting she's murdered him? That's too dramatic for words.'

'I'm not suggesting anything of the sort,' Mrs Henderson said defensively 'But supposing he's died naturally and she's just made off. He always kept a great deal of cash in the flat,' she added as if to clinch the argument.

'I'm sure you'll do what you think best,' Mrs Fox remarked with no great conviction.

'It's a question of one's duty.'

'Of course.'

'I'll find out if the caretaker knows anything and I'll also try to catch Mr Welling, though I doubt whether he'll know any more than you do.'

She turned briskly on her heel, leaving Mrs Fox staring after her with a bemused expression.

Normally she was always in bed by eleven o'clock, but on this particular evening she sat up, determined to catch Mr Welling when he arrived home. It was shortly after midnight that she heard the soft sigh of the lift. She had been sitting with her front door ajar in order to hear any comings and goings.

Mr Welling was on the point of opening his door when she called out to him.

'I'm so glad I happened to hear you come in, Mr Welling. I'm very worried about Mr Gray. Do you know what's happened to him? I've been trying to get in touch with him ever since I arrived home this afternoon, but there's no reply and I can't think what can have happened.'

As she spoke she moved across the landing to join Mr Welling outside his own door. He was a small dapper man in his forties who was always immaculately dressed whether in formal or casual attire. On this occasion he was wearing a pearl-grey suit with a pink shirt and a pink and grey striped tie. He seemed neither surprised nor annoyed at being pounced upon by his neighbour.

'I've no idea,' he said after a longish pause, 'but I'm sure there's no need to worry.'

'Have you seen his housekeeper at all during the past few days?'

'I can't say I have. Maybe she's gone away and—'

'And left Mr Gray to fend for himself?' Mrs Henderson enquired scathingly.

'I wasn't going to say that, though in fact I'm sure Mr Gray could well look after himself for a short while.'

'I'm certain something's happened to him. Anyway, I'd have known if Mrs Berry was going away. I'd offered to go in and sleep at his flat myself if need be. They both knew that.'

'But I believe you were away yourself over the weekend. They mightn't have wanted to mention it in case you felt you should alter your own arrangements.'

Mrs Henderson pondered the suggestion before dismissing it.

9

'I can't believe that for a moment,' she said.

'I imagine you've already spoken to Mrs Fox?'

'Yes. She doesn't know anything, either.'

'And the caretaker? Have you had a word with him?'

'I'm afraid Mr Bishop was as unhelpful as I've always found him. He just said it was none of his business. If you ask me, it's time we had a new caretaker.'

Mr Welling smiled in a noncommittal fashion, but made no comment other than to push his door open.

'A new day will doubtless bring fresh light,' he remarked as he stepped across his threshold.

'If it doesn't, I shall phone the police first thing in the morning. Somebody's got to do something. The poor man may be lying there dead.'

'In that event, he'll be the last person to be worrying.'

Mrs Henderson ignored the remark and, bidding Arthur Welling a tight-lipped goodnight, returned to her flat.

Despite her preoccupation with Mr Gray's fate, she slept soundly. She was fond of telling people that she always slept well because she had a clear conscience, implying that the reverse applied to anyone who passed a restless night.

At half-past seven the next morning she once more crossed the landing to Mr Gray's door. The paper-boy had already made his round, and a copy of the *Daily Telegraph* was sticking out of the letter-box. If there'd been anyone at home, it would have been removed by now. She knew that Mr Gray woke early and liked to read the paper in bed as soon as it arrived.

She prised out the newspaper and pushed the letter-flap open to peer inside. The kitchen door looked exactly as it had the previous afternoon, but more significant was the door of Janet Berry's room, which was in precisely the same half-closed position as she had previously noted it. There was neither sound nor scent of life within. It was time to alert the police.

Back in her own flat, she phoned the police station and when somebody asked her name and how he could help her she said without further preliminary: 'I want you to send an officer round to Southview Court. I'm afraid something's happened to Mr Gray in the flat opposite mine and I'm very worried.'

10

'So what is it you want the police to do, madam?' the voice enquired with well-practised patience.

'Go in and find out what's happened, of course.'

'We can't go breaking into people's homes without good cause.'

'I've told you...'

'How do you know the gentleman hasn't been called away?'

'He'd have left me a note. Anyway, I'm quite certain something's happened. Something to warrant police action. It's your duty to do something,' she added firmly.

A heavy sigh came down the line. 'All right, madam, I'll get somebody to call round, but I'm not making any promises about forcing an entry into this gentleman's flat.'

'But you're always breaking into people's homes,' Mrs Henderson expostulated. 'One's constantly reading about it in the papers. There's no point in one of your officers coming here and staring at Mr Gray's front door.'

'Someone'll be round, madam. I take it you'll be in?'

'I'll be waiting. Please don't let there be any delay.'

Forty minutes later there was a ring at her front door and she hurried to open it.

'Mrs Henderson?' a fair-haired uniformed sergeant with a clipped military moustache enquired.

'Yes. That's Mr Gray's flat across the landing.' She pointed eagerly over his shoulder, past the young woman police constable who was standing behind him.

He received the information with a brief nod, but didn't turn his head. 'Perhaps we could have a word with you first, Mrs Henderson. Then we'll decide what to do. I'm Sergeant York and this is WPC Hall.'

Seated in her living room with an attentive audience of two, Mrs Henderson recited the facts, throwing in a few observations about her less than helpful neighbours.

'So you see I have good reason for fearing that something must have happened to Mr Gray,' she concluded.

'Do you know whether anybody has a key to his flat?' Sergeant York asked.

'As far as I know only Mr Gray himself and Mrs Berry. I did once ask him if he would like me to have one just in case, but that was before Mrs Berry arrived on the scene.' Mrs

11

Henderson's tone expressed her feelings on both matters.

'Does he have any relatives you know of?'

'No. He's a wealthy old man alone in the world. His only visitors were myself and his solicitor from London, a Miss Epton.'

'I see. Well, I think that's all we need ask you for the moment, Mrs Henderson.' After a slight pause he added: 'In the light of what we discover, I may need to question you further.'

'I can assure you of my fullest co-operation,' she said briskly.

'Good! Then, let's go to Mr Gray's flat.'

After carefully examining the door for marks, Sergeant York peered through the letter-box, then sniffed at the air inside.

'Let's see if we can get in without making too much mess,' he said, straightening up.

He fetched a bunch of keys from his pocket, together with a length of narrow plastic. Turning his back on Mrs Henderson, he gave his attention once more to the door.

'Our locks are said to be burglar-proof,' Mrs Henderson remarked as she tried to see what he was doing.

'There's no such thing,' he remarked with a grunt.

A couple of minutes later there was a sudden click, followed by two more, and he pushed the door open. Mrs Henderson made to follow him in.

'You wait here, madam,' he said firmly.

'That's Mr Gray's bedroom,' she said, pointing at a closed door at the end of the passage to their right.

Standing by the front door like an eager but obedient dog awaiting its master's call, she watched the two officers move methodically from room to room. Mr Gray's bedroom was the last to be reached, and they disappeared inside, pushing the door to behind them. It seemed an age before either of them reappeared, while Mrs Henderson stood chafing outside. Eventually, WPC Hall emerged from the room and beckoned to her.

'I'm afraid your friend is dead,' she said gently. 'Sergeant York would like you to identify the body.'

'Of course,' Mrs Henderson said with a gulp as she followed

the girl back into the room.

Sergeant York was standing at the foot of the bed, and they both watched intently as Mrs Henderson peered at the head resting on the pillows.

She swung round abruptly and, in a tone both indignant and accusing, said: 'That's not Mr Gray. I've never seen this person before in my life.'

CHAPTER 2

Rosa Epton, junior partner in the firm of Snaith & Epton, solicitors, of west London, decided that she had chosen well over her new office carpet. It was steel blue in colour and, though she had had moments of doubt about it, her reservations had now been dispelled. Stephanie, their receptionist, telephonist and general Girl Friday, had been right all along about its attractiveness. It made the room seem both lighter and larger.

It had been Robin, her senior partner, who had suggested that the firm's profits that year justified the recarpeting of their suite of rooms.

'Let's tart ourselves up a bit,' he had said.

He had chosen burgundy red for his own room, and Stephanie had opted for mid-brown for everywhere else.

'So as not to show the coffee stains,' Ben, their young clerk, had observed.

Rosa slowly lifted her gaze from her new carpet and let it roam across the files on her desk. Some were more pressing than others – and more worrisome, too. She was particularly troubled by the case involving someone called Philip Tresant, even though it involved only minor theft. The allegation was that Tresant, a pillar of his church and local community, had stolen five pounds from the collection-plate at the end of a Sunday-morning service.

Rosa had not found him an easy client. He was a prickly, repressed man to whom communication didn't come naturally. Moreover, her subsequent discreet enquiries into his background were anything but encouraging. They showed him to be a lifelong kleptomaniac, who had managed to stay out of previous trouble through the loyalty of family and friends, who had been prepared to close ranks about him whenever necessary.

'He needs psychiatric treatment,' his distraught wife had said to Rosa. 'If he's convicted, it'll be the end of our lives,' she had gone on tearfully. 'The children will have to leave their schools and we could never face the neighbours again.'

It was clear to Rosa that Jean Tresant believed her husband to be guilty, despite his staunch denials to his solicitor.

It was later that Rosa learnt he had been a petty pilferer all his life. From other boys' lockers at school, from clothing left in the tennis club changing room, and from colleagues' desks in the office. Cigarettes, small sums of money, almost anything that could be slipped into a pocket.

It seemed that he had been suspected before of stealing from the collection-plate, but nobody had wished to provoke a scandal. Eventually, however, a fellow-sidesman, one Gerald Provis, had been so outraged at seeing him pinch a five-pound note that he had accused him to his face. Philip Tresant had gone very white and had left the vestry without saying a word. Later he was to deny the accusation and say that the other man had never liked him and had acted out of malice. Recriminations reached the point where his accuser had said that if nobody else would act, then he would and he went to the police.

It might be thought that enough damage had already been done to both their reputations, but positions became entrenched, with people wringing their hands and being forced to take sides.

By the time Tresant consulted Rosa, the die was cast and he was awaiting trial in the local magistrates' court.

Rosa had never felt she had to like her clients, though it certainly helped when she did. Equally, belief in their innocence was unimportant. In fact it was better not to become emotionally involved in their cause.

From the outset she found Philip Tresant an awkward client, reserved and at the same time priggish. On his very first visit to the office, she had had to go out of the room for a few minutes and had returned to find he had obviously disturbed the papers on her desk. It had not been a good start to their relationship, and she had been in two minds about

15

accepting him as a client. But he had sensed her hostility and had immediately sought to charm her in his own clumsy way.

When Rosa had asked him how he had come to consult *her*, he had replied that he hadn't wanted a local solicitor and that he had seen Rosa's name in a west-London paper which someone had left on the seat next to his on the Underground.

Clients arrived at Snaith & Epton's door in all manner of ways and there was nothing particularly implausible about Philip Tresant's introduction to the firm. Take old Mr Vernon Gray, for example. He had seen Rosa on television and thought she was the only member of a panel of lawyers who spoke sense and had written to her to say so. She still had his letter of a year ago. It was the first in what was now a fairly voluminous file.

Dear Miss Epton,
I saw you on television last night in the programme 'Legal Aid'. While your colleagues patronised us with their legal clichés, you were the only person on the panel who spoke plain English and showed a human touch. The fellow next to you talked more high-falutin gibber-ish than all the rest, and I suspect you thought so, too.

As you will see from my address I live on the south coast and am myself in need of the services of a solicitor at this moment. For various reasons, I prefer not to consult anyone locally and hope that you will accept me as a client. I went to the public library this morning and looked you up in a lawyers' reference-book. I mention that as you may wonder how I know the name of your firm and its address.

May I hope for a favourable reply?

Yours sincerely,
VERNON GRAY

PS As you won't find me in any reference-book, perhaps I should mention that I am retired and seventy-nine years old. I have been a widower for twenty years.

16

Rosa pondered this letter on and off for several days, uncertain how to reply. Personal and professional courtesy required her to answer it in some way, if only to thank him for his comments on her television appearance, but to turn him away as a client. There was a lack of subtlety about the letter that affronted her. On the other hand, she was intrigued. Had it not been for the disarming postscript, however, she might well have told him to look elsewhere for a solicitor, in the belief that he was seeking something rather cosier than legal advice. But if he was a seventy-nine-year-old widower, it seemed unlikely that he had merely fallen for her face.

In the event she waited three days before writing and thanking him for his kind remarks about her appearance, adding that, if he cared to tell her the nature of the legal services he was in need of, she would let him know whether they fell within her competence.

By return came a letter saying that he wanted advice on making a will, having never previously made one, and also that he was being prosecuted for driving without due care and attention after colliding with a lamp-post.

Rosa held firm views about people who didn't make wills when they had something to leave; also about old men (or women) driving cars when unsafe to do so. Accordingly she wrote and said she would be pleased to see him if he cared to phone and make an appointment.

His reply, however, made her wonder if she had not fallen into a trap.

Dear Miss Epton,
I thank you for your letter accepting me as a client. I shall be grateful, however, if you will visit me at my home, as my health precludes a journey to London. I would naturally pay for the additional time involved, as well as your travelling expenses. I shall be delighted to give you lunch in a pleasant restaurant just round the corner from here.

Let me know which day next week would suit you.

Your sincerely,
VERNON GRAY

PS My appearance in the magistrates' court has been put off for several weeks.

Rosa felt distinctly cross at this turn of events. However, when she showed the letter to her partner, Robin Snaith, he merely laughed and said: 'A day in Mongton's no great hardship, even if you subsequently decline to act for him. Anyway, he sounds a spirited old boy. It could be a day of adventure. And there's always lunch.'

'I have no intention of having lunch with him, that's for sure,' Rosa said firmly. 'If I go, I shall arrive after lunch.'

Which is exactly what she did. She caught a fast train from Victoria just after one o'clock and had a toasted sandwich in the buffet, washed down with British Rail coffee. From the station she took a taxi to Southview Court where she arrived at a quarter past two. As she pressed the bell she reflected that she would soon know whether her decision to come had been foolishly quixotic.

The door opened so suddenly that she was taken by surprise, as she hadn't heard any approaching footsteps. The explanation was soon apparent – a thick carpet and her host's bedroom slippers.

'Come in, Miss Epton,' he said, standing aside for her to enter. 'That's the living room on the right,' he added, pointing, as he closed the front door behind her. He followed her into the room and waved vaguely at a selection of chairs.

'I always sit there,' he went on, indicating an upright winged armchair.

Rosa selected a chair and sat down and covertly studied her host for the first time. He was tall and thin with a slight stoop. His face was lined, and he had receding white hair brushed straight back from his forehead. His mouth turned down at the corners and gave his face an unyielding, stubborn expression. He didn't look the sort of person to write fan letters to people he had seen on television. At least, not without an ulterior motive.

She glanced round the room, which was expensively furnished. Venetian blinds were partially lowered, diffusing the late-autumn sunshine.

'I live on my own,' he said, 'but I've made coffee if you'd like some.'

18

'No, thank you, I had some on the train.' She leant forward. 'Let's talk about the two matters you mentioned in your letter.'

'Certainly. Which first?' he asked, giving her a hint of a smile.

'Tell me about the motoring offence.'

He took some documents from the small table beside him and handed them to her.

'There's the summons and a couple of letters from the court.'

Rosa cast a quick expert eye over them. 'If you're convicted,' she said, 'the court will almost certainly take away your licence until you pass a driving test. Will that be a great hardship?'

'Not a bit. I've already decided not to drive again. I'm in the process of selling my car.'

'That certainly makes things much easier. Do I take it, therefore, you're proposing to plead guilty?'

'Whatever you advise, Miss Epton.'

'I can't advise you until I know the facts. What exactly happened?'

From his recital of events, it was apparent that he had no defence and that a plea of guilty was inevitable. An unoffending lamp-post had been demolished when his car mounted a central reservation and gave it a buffet that left it tilting at an angle of forty-five degrees. Fortunately, nobody had been hurt apart from Mr Gray himself, who suffered some superficial bruising.

'I'll let the court know that you will be pleading guilty and are not proposing to drive again,' she said, not a little irked that he had brought her all the way to Mongton on such a trivial matter. 'That, at least, should help to mitigate the penalty. And now the other matter. Are you telling me that you've never made a will in your life?'

'That's right.'

'And yet you obviously have assets to leave,' she went on.

'That's why I thought I'd better make one now.'

'Certainly better late than never,' Rosa observed crisply. 'Generally speaking, people who die intestate with a large estate to be distributed leave behind a good deal of heartache, if not resentment. Moreover, the avaricious Treasury comes

19

off better than it otherwise would – or deserves to.' She paused. 'If you really want the State to be a main beneficiary, it's still better to make a will and say so. I take it you have a list of people whom you wish to benefit by your will?'

He had listened to her attentively, but with an expression that gave nothing away. She almost wondered if he had taken in what she'd been saying.

'As I mentioned in my letter, Miss Epton, I've been a widower for twenty years, and my wife and I never had any children.'

'Do you have any living brothers and sisters?'

'I have a brother in Australia, but I'm not sure if he's still alive. We lost touch years ago.'

'Would he, assuming he's still alive, be your closest relative?'

'I suppose he would.'

'Then, if you died intestate, he would be the main beneficiary. Does he have any children?'

'Two daughters.'

'Are they married?'

'Several times over, I believe.'

'With children?'

'Yes, but don't ask me how many.'

'Well, Mr Gray, unless you make a will, they're the people who'll benefit by your death, assuming your brother's no longer alive. If you want your nieces and their offspring to inherit, it'd be much better that they do so under your will than by virtue of your intestacy.'

'I don't particularly want them to have anything,' he remarked, the corners of his mouth taking a disapproving dip.

'Then, who do you wish to leave your estate to?' Rosa asked with a note of exasperation.

'That's where I need your advice.'

She stared at him in cautious disbelief.

'I've never met you before today and you're asking me to advise you on something as personal as that?'

He nodded. 'And I'd like you to be an executor. As I told you in my letter, I was greatly impressed by your television appearance. I felt you were somebody I could trust and who would advise me impartially. And you had the additional

20

advantage of knowing nothing about me.'

Used as she was to eccentric clients with heads full of strange notions, this was pure *Alice in Wonderland*. And, like Lewis Carroll's Alice, Rosa found herself puzzled, exasperated and intrigued all at the same time.

'But you've got to give me some ideas,' she said at last. 'For example, do you have any pet charities?'

He shook his head impatiently.

'Any close friends?'

'One or two people drop by from time to time. Mrs Henderson in the flat opposite is my most frequent visitor. She'd make me one of her good causes if I let her.'

'Would you propose leaving her something in your will?'

'I could leave her five hundred pounds, I suppose,' he said offhandedly. 'Even a thousand. She's been kind to me in her own bossy way.' From the way he spoke, he might have been sorting out the loose change in his trouser pocket.

'Who else?' Rosa enquired drily.

'Nobody in this block. Unless I left a small sum to provide earplugs for everyone who lives within hearing of Mrs Fox. She also has a flat on this floor. She fancies herself as a singer. I once told her I'd heard more music coming out of the parrot house at the zoo, and she's never forgiven me. You're lucky, she seems to be out this afternoon.' His tone was acerbic and devoid of any note of tolerance. 'The only other person on this floor', he went on, 'is a man called Welling, and I certainly don't intend leaving him anything. He's a club-owner and probably has more than the rest of us put together. Anyway, I scarcely know him.'

Rosa took a deep breath. 'What's the approximate value of your estate?' she asked.

'Probably about £300,000, including this flat.'

'I see,' she said in a thoughtful tone. She felt totally nonplussed by their conversation, the more so as she had failed to divine what was really passing through his mind. After a slightly oppressive silence, she said: 'Well, Mr Gray, I can only advise you to make a will as soon as possible; but, first, you have to decide on your beneficiaries – £500 to Mrs Henderson is hardly a foundation on which to construct a will. I suggest you give the matter immediate and serious

21

thought and then call me when you've decided what you want to do.'

'And you'll be an executor?'

'If you really want that, but I suggest you have a second executor who should be someone who knows you personally. There must be such a person.' Rosa got up.

'Thank you for coming, Miss Epton.' He fumbled in his pocket and pulled out a folded cheque. 'This is for £250 to cover your expenses et cetera, and as a token of my good intentions.' When Rosa hesitated, he went on: 'No, please take it. I'm not trying to bribe you. Hold it on account.'

It was with some effort that he got up from his chair. Observing him, it suddenly occurred to Rosa to ask him a question.

'Do you have a regular doctor?'

'Dr Nagy. He's Hungarian. Came here during the 1956 troubles in his country. Obliging sort of chap and a good doctor as far as I'm concerned.'

'Do you see him often?'

'Not more than I need. I suffer from high blood-pressure, for which I have to take tablets, and he likes to see me for a check-up every three months.' He paused and gazed thoughtfully out of the window. 'I wouldn't mind leaving him something in my will. I'm glad you mentioned him.'

'What about asking him to be an executor?'

'Do I need to ask him?'

'It's a question of courtesy. Also, if you appoint him without getting his permission, he might refuse to act. Executors have that right.'

'I don't expect he'd refuse if I left him a large enough legacy.'

'It'd still be better to approach him first,' Rosa said tartly. 'Anyway, think about it and let me know as soon as you've made up your mind.'

So ended Rosa's first visit to Mr Gray. As she travelled back to London she felt she wouldn't mind if it were her last. It wasn't just that he was eccentric but the near-certainty that he was going to prove a tiresome client that weighed with her. The very next day, however, she was surprised to find a letter from him sitting on her desk when she came in. He must have

22

sat down and written it immediately after her departure.

Dear Miss Epton,

It was very good of you to come down and see me, and I sincerely hope you're not having any second thoughts about accepting me as a client.

I have carefully considered all you said about making a will and I have decided I will leave everything to Dr Nagy. It'll probably come as something of a surprise to him, but what does that matter and anyway I shan't be around to know. Obviously I shan't tell him – not that I think it would encourage him to hasten my end. He's a good man and has a nice German wife whom I've met once. Apart from him, my only other bequests are £500 to Mrs Henderson and £500 to yourself if you will act as my executor.

You're every bit as impressive in person as you appeared to be on the small screen.

I look forward to hearing from you.

Yours sincerely,
VERNON GRAY

'What do you think I ought to do, Robin?' she asked her partner after giving him the letter to read. 'I mean, here he is proposing to leave the whole of his not inconsiderable estate to somebody he'd never even thought of until I innocently asked him if he had a doctor.'

Robin nodded slowly. 'I'd phone him and make sure it really is what he wants. Record the conversation so that you're covered in the event of any trouble later on.' He paused. 'You've no reason to think he's not of sound mind and therefore incapable of making a will?'

'I almost wish I did.' She sighed. 'I don't want to dump him. On the other hand, I feel he's going to cause more bother than he's worth.'

'You'd better think twice before you appear on television again. But, seriously, I don't know why you can't just accept him as another client. If we get too fastidious about whom we will or won't act for, we'll go out of business. We're not required to love or even like all our clients, let alone believe in the justice of their causes....'

'I know, I know.'

'And it's not as if your Mr Gray can't pay for your services.' Observing Rosa's still worried expression, he went on: 'People have made odder wills than his. At least his doctor is a worthier cause than some outlandish society for the protection of camels in Arabia.'

'OK, I'll do as you suggest,' Rosa said, her mind apparently made up. 'And I must confess to being intrigued by the old boy.'

When later that day she called Mr Gray he confirmed that those indeed were his wishes and he thanked Rosa warmly for having focused his mind on the terms of his will. In the event she found herself agreeing to take the document down to Mongton for his signature when it had been prepared.

'You'll need two witnesses who are not beneficiaries,' she said. 'Can you arrange that?'

'If you let me take you out to lunch this time, we can get a couple of waiters to do it,' he said airily.

Thus it was that Rosa caught the train to Mongton one day the following week, carrying in her briefcase the last will and testament of Vernon Gray. She had made it clear to him that her prompt return was solely motivated by the urgent desirability of his having a valid will in existence. She didn't wish him to think that she was secretly chafing to see him again so soon.

On this occasion he met her at the station in a hired car and they drove immediately to the restaurant. Then, after a carefully chosen meal, they retired to the manager's office where the head waiter and a motherly cloakroom lady duly witnessed the signing of the will, for which brief service they were generously tipped. Rosa had attended a good many curious occasions in her professional career, but this one struck her as bizarre as any.

She had intended returning to London immediately afterwards, but was persuaded to go back to his flat. She was made to feel that it would be churlish to dash off at once to the station.

She was still in two minds about the wisdom of having accepted the old man as a client, despite all Robin had said, but now she seemed to have committed herself. Short of his asking her to do something outrageous, he had, for better or for worse, become what Robin jocularly chose to call 'a real paying customer'. Moreover, he had been a kind and thoughtful host at lunch – not that she felt she knew him any better by the end of the meal than before their first meeting. She increasingly had the impression that part of him lay behind a high unscalable wall. He talked knowledgeably about what was happening in the world, but told her very little about himself. She gathered he had been an accountant, but beyond that broad bare fact he vouchsafed nothing of his past. It seemed he had been a widower so long that he had almost forgotten he'd ever had a wife. She certainly played no part in his conversation other than as a sort of milestone, rather the way people use historical events as reference-points.

Her third visit came some weeks later when she travelled down to defend him on the motoring charge. This was something of a formality, and Rosa felt that the penalty (a £100 fine, £250 costs and the loss of his licence) would have been the same whatever she had said, or even if she'd not been there to say anything at all.

With the case over and his will made, she hoped he would become one of those clients whose affairs would remain dormant for a while.

It was a hope not to be fulfilled.

Some three weeks after the court hearing she received a phone call from Dr Nagy saying that Mr Gray had suffered a small stroke and was under observation in a private nursing home. He was anxious that his solicitor should visit him as he thought he might not have long to live. Dr Nagy added his own opinion that, despite his patient's age, there was no reason why he shouldn't make a reasonable recovery.

Two days later a somewhat reluctant Rosa went to see him. She found him sitting in a chair in his room with a plaid rug wrapped round his legs. His speech was slightly slurred, and she gathered he was partially paralysed down his left side.

Though he expressed pleasure at seeing her, he didn't

25

seem to have anything special he wanted to say. Rosa decided that the two days since Dr Nagy had phoned had given him fresh hope of living.

Knowing that the doctor was named an executor in his will, Rosa took the opportunity of asking Mr Gray whether he had yet sought the doctor's consent to the appointment. Mr Gray shook his head.

'He'll act all right,' he said with a trace of impatience.

He probably would, too, Rosa reflected wryly, when he learnt of what would turn out to be a totally unexpected inheritance.

She was about to say goodbye and leave when the door flew open and a woman came bustling in.

'Oh! I didn't know you already had a visitor,' she exclaimed in a vexed tone on seeing Rosa.

'It's all right, I'm just about to go.'

'I'm Olive Henderson. I'm a neighbour of Mr Gray. I'm keeping an eye on his flat for him.'

'This is my solicitor, Miss Epton,' Mr Gray said in a quietly complacent tone.

'I thought you probably were,' Mrs Henderson remarked. Turning to him, she went on: 'I've brought you some soup, made from real stock. It's got far more nourishment in it than anything they'll give you here.' She turned back to Rosa. 'Don't let me hold you up, Miss Epton.' Then, lowering her voice, she added: 'And, if there's anything I can do, you only have to ask me.'

About a week later, Dr Nagy phoned Rosa again and said that Mr Gray was fit enough to be discharged, but ought to have a live-in housekeeper.

'He'd like you to find someone suitable, Miss Epton,' he concluded.

'I imagine that's rather easier said than done,' Rosa said in a resigned tone.

'I could find him a trained nurse, but he doesn't need professional care of that sort. All he requires is a sensible woman who will look after him and undertake the domestic chores.' He paused before adding: 'I suggested that his neighbour, Mrs Henderson, would probably be willing to find someone, but he was most definite that he didn't want her *interfering*, as he put it.'

26

Thirty years in England had given Dr Nagy a command of colloquial and almost accentless English. She gathered he had only just qualified as a doctor when he fled his country. He and Rosa hadn't met yet, but were bound to do so sooner or later.

With this phone call began the most exhausting and frustrating period of her professional relationship with her egregious client. After vetting a number of applications for the post of housekeeper, Rosa travelled down to Mongton so that they could together interview the two most promising on paper and select the better.

Three weeks later, however, Rosa received a brief letter from the woman they had eventually chosen saying that she would be leaving at the end of the month. She hinted that her employer was a disagreeable old man who was impossible to please. When Rosa phoned Mr Gray to give him the news, he simply said: 'Good riddance.'

Over the next eight months three more came and went, to Rosa's increasing frustration. By then she had come to the conclusion that her client was primarily to blame for this rapid turnover, though she suspected that Mrs Henderson was not blameless. On two occasions she had taken it upon herself to phone Rosa and inform her that the current occupant was quite unsuitable and should be replaced.

'I know what I'm talking about, Miss Epton,' she had said. 'I've had a lot of experience of these so-called housekeepers and I assure you they need very careful selection. Most of them are useless. I'll be very willing to help you interview the next.'

As far as Rosa was concerned she was more than welcome to take on the responsibility, but Mr Gray's reaction was immediate.

'Have pity on me, Miss Epton! She'd find me someone in her mould. I know I'm a bit difficult at times, but don't throw me to the wolves.'

Rosa thought it might be the wolves who retired hurt.

She had almost lost count of all the women she'd inter-viewed when Janet Berry moved in at the end of June. Rosa detected an underlying seam of toughness beneath her somewhat taciturn manner. She assured Rosa that she was used to coping with awkward employers and didn't let them upset her. Her taciturnity also seemed a bonus, as Mr Gray had complained that some of the previous ones had never stopped talking. Even so, the fact that he gave Mrs Berry his own stamp of approval wasn't by itself a cause for optimism. He had approved each one in turn, but sooner or later disenchantment always set in on one side or the other.

But, when three months went by without any serious complaints either way, Rosa was filled with cautious hope that at last they'd found the right person. Admittedly, Mr Gray had on one or two occasions said he didn't care for Mrs Berry's manner, but when pressed had been forced to agree that she performed her duties satisfactorily.

'I just don't much care for her,' he had said querulously when speaking to Rosa on the phone.

'But she does her work all right?'

'Yes, I suppose so.'

'She's a good cook?'

'Yes,' he said, albeit grudgingly.

'And she keeps the place clean?'

'Yes.'

'And is always around when you want her?'

'All right, there's no need to go on. All I said was that I didn't much care for her. She's a bit offhand at times. And she was rude to Mrs Henderson the other day,' he added with a touch of malice.

'I take it you wouldn't want to give her the sack on that account.'

'When are you coming down to see me again?' he asked, changing the subject with customary abruptness when he wasn't getting anywhere.

'I'm completely tied up at the moment, but I'll call you next week. Meanwhile, be nice to Mrs Berry. You're lucky to have her.'

'One day you'll be sorry you ever said that,' he observed in a tone that Rosa realised was intended to make her feel guilty. To that extent she knew him too well, even if she still often felt she hardly knew him at all.

It was about a week later that Rosa returned from court one afternoon to be informed by Stephanie that the Mongton police had been trying to get in touch with her.

'A Sergeant York would like you to call him.'

'Did he say what about?'

'No, but I imagine it's to do with Mr Gray. Who else?'

'Who else indeed?' Rosa said with a sigh. 'I wonder what's happened now.'

'Shall I get Sergeant York on the phone?'

'I suppose you'd better.'

She had barely reached her room when the phone buzzed and Stephanie announced that Sergeant York was on the line.

'Miss Epton? Sergeant York, Mongton police, here. I understand that Mr Gray of Southview Court is a client of yours?'

'Yes, he is.'

'Do you have any idea where he is?'

'If he's not at home, then I have no idea.'

'He seems to have disappeared,' Sergeant York said bleakly. 'One of his neighbours became anxious at not being able to get any answer at his flat and called us.'

Rosa felt she had no need to ask which neighbour.

'He has a housekeeper....'

'She's disappeared, too.'

'I can't think what can have happened to him. I spoke to him on the phone about a week ago, but he never mentioned anything about going away.' Rosa paused and, choosing her words carefully, went on: 'Is there any reason for thinking some harm may have befallen him?'

'Only the presence of an unidentified dead man in his bed. And *he'd* certainly not died a natural death.'

'Good gracious! You really mean you have no idea whose body it is?'

'It could be the Man in the Moon for all we know at the moment.'

'Do you mean that all the usual means of identification are missing?'

'Precisely.'

'I'd better come down,' Rosa said hesitantly, 'though I'm not sure what use I can be.'

'I'm not too sure, either, Miss Epton, but I think you should. For the time being Mr Gray and Mrs Berry are merely missing persons, but that situation could change at

29

any moment.' He paused. 'Has Mrs Henderson been in touch with you?'

'No.'

'Good! I told her to leave it to the police, but I thought she'd try to be first with the news. I take it you know the lady?'

'I've met her,' Rosa said in a neutral tone.

'And Mr Gray's other neighbours?'

'I know them only by hearsay. I don't think Mr Gray was on particularly friendly terms with either Mrs Fox or Mr Welling.'

Sergeant York made no comment and shortly afterwards rang off.

Rosa stared pensively at her desk calendar for a while. It showed Wednesday, 9 October, a date she was to remember for a long time.

CHAPTER 3

'How on earth does a strange body find its way into your client's bed?' Robin exclaimed when Rosa told him what had happened.

'You may well ask.'

'It's totally bizarre.'

'I agree.'

'Surely the police have some idea as to what happened?'

'They appear not to.'

'Well, they're bound to by the time you get down there tomorrow. Meanwhile, what's happened to your old boy? It's a bit sinister, he and his housekeeper vanishing like that. One can only hope he's still alive. My guess is that Janet Berry is mixed up in some criminal enterprise or other. How much do you really know about her?'

'I took up the references she supplied, and they were perfectly satisfactory.'

'References are easily forged.'

'I know; but the fact remains she's lasted longer than any of her predecessors. Though, I suppose, that in itself can be regarded as suspicious.'

'It's the body in the bed that gives the whole thing a touch of Grand Guignol.'

Rosa nodded. 'If it were a neighbour or the milkman, it wouldn't be half as intriguing.'

'Can one assume', Robin said in a speculative tone, 'that Mr Gray and Mrs Berry must have known about the body before they disappeared?'

'Only if one accepts the inference that they put it in the bed themselves.' Rosa sighed. 'I just hope the police will have identified the corpse by the time I arrive tomorrow.'

'Even if they have, it won't necessarily resolve the other half of the puzzle, namely what's happened to your client.'

Rosa accepted that as self-evident. She was already persuaded that Vernon Gray was a wily and devious old man, without his sudden unexplained disappearance. It was a view which had been fortified on each occasion she had visited him. Robin broke in on her thoughts.

'How are you fixed tomorrow? Anything I can take off your shoulders?'

'Thanks, Robin, but I've managed to clear my decks. I did have Philip Tresant coming in the afternoon for another agonising conference, but his wife phoned only an hour ago to say he was unwell and wouldn't be able to make it.'

'When does his case come up?'

'The week after next. We've got nothing further to talk about, but he seems to think that unless he comes along here once a week I shall forget all about him. I rather wish I could. He's another client I could have done without. I just feel terribly sorry for his wife and children, whom I've never met. If I don't get him off, I dread to think what his wife may do.'

'There's no chance of his pleading guilty and hurling himself on the psychiatrist's couch?'

'None. If anything, I'm his psychiatrist. You should see the way he drifts about my room when he's here. He picks up files from my desk as if they're magazines in a dentist's waiting room.'

'Do you still think you can get him off on the facts?'

'I'm going to have a damned good try,' Rosa said vigorously. 'I gather his accuser is by no means invulnerable, which provides some hope.'

Robin never ceased to marvel that someone so small and feminine could exude so much determination at the scent of forensic contest.

'Well, good luck at Mongton tomorrow,' he said. 'Call me at home in the evening if I don't see you back here first.'

'At the moment I've no idea how long I'll be there.'

'I'd be prepared for a long day.'

It was a few minutes after ten o'clock the next morning when Rosa walked into the police station and asked for Sergeant

York. He appeared almost as quickly as if she had rubbed a magic lamp and summoned him.

'Had any news of Mr Gray?' he asked before Rosa had time to put the same question to him.

'None. And I assume you haven't, either.'

'We're no further forward than when I spoke to you yesterday.'

'You still haven't identified the body in the bed?'

'No. Perhaps you wouldn't mind looking at some photographs, Miss Epton. Let's go to my office. Actually, it's the inspector's office, but he's away and it'll be easier to talk there than in the hubbub of the room where I have a desk.'

They reached the office and he pulled up a chair for Rosa. Then, picking up a folder, he took out a number of photographs.

'You're not squeamish about mortuary photographs, are you, Miss Epton?'

'I've seen my share of them,' Rosa said with a faint smile.

'Here we are, then,' he said, handing them to her.

The first showed a man of indeterminate age lying on his back on a mortuary table. He was naked and his skin had a white etiolated appearance. The second photograph showed a close-up of his face. The eyes were closed, and he had an ill-shaven look. His hair was more grey than not and had receded at the sides. The next two photographs were of the back of his head. One revealed a patch of blood-clotted hair, the other showed the same area after it had been shaved.

Aware that Sergeant York was watching her intently, Rosa looked up.

'I've never seen him before in my life,' she said. 'But that's hardly surprising, seeing that I never met any of Mr Gray's friends or acquaintances.'

'Did he ever mention anyone who could have resembled this guy?'

'No. He always gave the impression of being without any real friends or even close acquaintances.'

'How old would you say this man was?'

'Surely the pathologist is the person to tell you that.'

'I'd still like to hear your guess.'

'I would say he's somebody who hasn't worn very well and is

33

younger than he looks. Not that mortuary photographs are ever particularly flattering! I'd say he was in his late thirties, but looks at least ten years older than that.' She paused. 'Somehow he doesn't look at rest, even in death.'

'The pathologist reckons he's about forty, so you're spot on, Miss Epton.'

'Have you shown these photographs to anyone else?'

'To everybody we can think of who might conceivably recognise him. To all the residents at Southview Court, to the postman, the milkman, the candlestick-maker, the lot. We've drawn a total blank.'

'None of them has ever seen him before?'

'None of them admits to doing so,' Sergeant York said carefully. Rosa shot him a quick glance, and he went on: 'We suspect that one person is not being totally frank with us.'

'Any point in my asking who that person is?'

'If I tell you, Miss Epton, it's because I hope it may assist your own recollection.' He frowned and scratched the end of his nose. 'I had the impression – and it was no more than an impression – that Mr Welling was lying when he said he had never seen this man before.'

He raised his eyebrows and gave Rosa a hopeful look.

'I'm afraid it doesn't help me to recall anything. I've only seen Mr Welling once in my life and then we did no more than exchange a good-morning. He was coming out of his front door on one occasion when I was arriving to visit Mr Gray.'

'Did Mr Gray ever talk about him?'

'Never. They may have lived on the same floor of the same block, but they occupied separate worlds.'

'What about Mrs Berry – did she ever mention him?'

'No. As you've probably found out, Mr Gray had little to do with any of his neighbours save for Mrs Henderson, who rather thrust herself at him.'

'She's a thrusting sort of lady,' Sergeant York observed. 'In one sense it's unfortunate that all this happened when she was away for the weekend. If she'd been at home, she might well have spotted something amiss.'

'I wonder if it really was a coincidence that it all happened during her absence,' Rosa said in a thoughtful voice.

'You think it may have been deliberately planned that way?'
Sergeant York said in a startled tone.

'It's probably no more than a far-fetched thought, but it
may be worth bearing in mind.' After a pause she went on:
'What gave you the impression that Mr Welling wasn't
speaking the truth when he said he'd never seen the dead
man before?'

'It was his expression when I showed him the photograph.
Surprise, even alarm, but almost immediately he recovered
his composure.'

'Which would seem to indicate that, although he recognised
the dead man, he wasn't aware of his death.'

'That's how I interpreted it.'

'Maybe the dead man had frequented one of Mr Welling's
clubs.'

'That's something we're looking into.' He paused. 'What
are you going to do about your client?'

'What can I do, except await events? Incidentally, who has a
key to his flat?'

'We had to break the lock to get in. Since then we've had a
fresh one fitted.' With a flicker of a smile he added: 'At Mr
Gray's expense, I'm afraid. The police are very cost-conscious
these days.'

'In that case, presumably I can have a key on my client's
behalf.'

'You're free to go to the flat, Miss Epton. We've finished
there.'

'You mean, you've completed all your tests? Incidentally,
what was the cause of death?'

Sergeant York pursed his lips. 'It's associated with the
injury to the back of his head. But the pathologist still has
further tests to make.'

'So the head injury wasn't the actual cause of death?'

'It mayn't have been. It seems he was also suffering from
some form of heart disease, which played a part.'

'So it could be anything from murder to accidental death?'

'Yes; that's why we're very anxious to trace Mr Gray and
Mrs Berry and establish exactly what did happen.' He fixed
Rosa with a severe look. 'Of course, the fact that they've
disappeared isn't in their favour.'

35

'Nor does it tell against them at this stage,' Rosa said. 'Without knowing a great deal more, one can't possibly start drawing conclusions.' She got up. 'Well, if you'll give me a key, I'll go to the flat. I only want to have a quick look around.'

'I must ask you not to remove anything, Miss Epton,' Sergeant York said with a trace of unease.

'I won't, though I doubt whether you have the law on your side to stop me. After all, you don't yet have evidence that a crime's been committed involving my client.'

'A dead man in his bed with head injuries requires an explanation,' Sergeant York observed tartly. 'Anyway, here's the key. Perhaps you'd be good enough to call me if you discover anything that might help solve the mystery.'

'I'm as anxious to find out what's happened to my client as you are,' Rosa said, sidestepping the request.

Mrs Fox showed no sign of having lost her voice as a result of the dramatic happenings on the sixth floor of Southview Court. She was singing lustily when Rosa stepped out of the lift, her fondness for fortissimo being more easily forgiven by somebody who didn't live next to her.

Rosa had barely turned the key in Mr Gray's lock when a door behind her opened and Mrs Henderson called out.

'I thought it must be you, Miss Epton. I'm glad you're here as I wanted to have a word with you. In fact I phoned your office this morning and was told you were on your way to Mongton. Would you like to come in for a cup of coffee and we can discuss things?'

Rosa hesitated a moment. A talk with Mrs Henderson might prove useful. Moreover, she felt she could do with a cup of coffee.

Mrs Henderson's flat reflected its owner. It was clinically tidy, but chock-a-block with possessions. There was a glass cabinet full of china knick-knacks and a table covered with family photographs in old-fashioned frames. Under the window was a chaise longue on which were neatly stacked piles of magazines, most of them with an apparently church flavour.

'I knew that Berry woman was no good,' Mrs Henderson called out from the kitchen where she was making the coffee.

'I wouldn't be surprised to learn she's been in trouble with the law. There was something sly about her. I never liked her from the start.'

Mr Gray would probably have considered this a recommendation, Rosa thought.

'Mr Gray seemed quite satisfied with her,' Rosa retorted with a touch of asperity. 'And she always seemed to be conscientious and efficient.'

'You didn't see as much of her as I did, Miss Epton. Unfortunately, Mr Gray chose to ignore what I told him. He could be most stubborn and wilful at times. But I did my best to warn him about her.'

'Warn him in what way?'

'About what she got up to after he'd gone to bed at nights. She used to go out and leave him and not return until the small hours. I don't call that being very *conscientious*, as you put it.'

'And you brought this to Mr Gray's attention?' Rosa enquired in a sly tone.

'Most certainly I did, but he brushed me aside and said that as long as nobody disturbed his sleep he didn't mind what they got up to.'

'She may even have gone out with his approval.'

'I'm quite sure he had no idea until I told him and then he was too obstinate to do anything about it. I was proposing to tell you the next time you came down, but this all happened first.' Mrs Henderson pursed her lips in disapproval as she went on: 'I caught her slipping out of his flat around half-past ten one night. She told me she had a headache and was going out for a breath of fresh air. A breath of fresh air, indeed! You don't need to put on lipstick and eyeshadow to get a breath of fresh air. Of course, I knew she was lying. She came back in a taxi at two o'clock accompanied by Mr Welling. It so happened that I hadn't been able to get to sleep and was standing at my bedroom window when they returned.'

'How long ago was this?'

'About three weeks. Since then I've heard her go out late on a number of occasions.'

'Well, if Mr Gray didn't mind, I don't really see why she shouldn't have. He didn't need her around him twenty-four

37

hours a day, and if he was already in bed—'

'I'm positive she was up to no good,' Mrs Henderson broke in.

Rosa was inclined to believe that Mrs Henderson regarded anyone as being up to mischief if they weren't at home by ten o'clock. As for actually going out at that hour. ... Nevertheless she was interested in the link between Janet Berry and Mr Welling that had been revealed. It might be perfectly innocent. Probably was. There was no reason why they shouldn't have enjoyed one another's company. If Mr Welling had ever had a wife, she was obviously no longer around, and Janet Berry had told Rosa that she herself was estranged from her husband. It took a Mrs Henderson to see something sinister in their relationship.

'I very much doubt if Mr Gray will ever be found alive,' Mrs Henderson now said in a matter-of-fact tone. 'If only I'd not gone away last weekend. You can imagine what a shock it's all been to me. I still can't get over seeing that dead man in Mr Gray's bed and the police assuming it was Mr Gray.'

'It must have been a great shock,' Rosa said as she envisaged the scene. 'Incidentally, have you told the police what you've just told me about Mr Welling and Mrs Berry?'

'I considered it my duty to tell them everything.' She paused. 'If you're going over to Mr Gray's flat, would you like me to come with you?'

Rosa shook her head. 'I'll just have a quick look around on my own.' Mrs Henderson was the last person she wanted at her side.

She closed Mr Gray's front door firmly behind her and stood for a moment in the silent hallway. Then she walked towards his half-open bedroom door and peered in. The bed was unmade and had a rumpled appearance. For a second she felt shocked, then reminded herself that the police hadn't come there to do the housework. None the less a cold unmade bed was a particularly sordid sight. She suddenly realised that the pillow was missing. Presumably the police had taken it away for laboratory examination.

She turned and walked towards the large living room at the further end of the flat. Mr Gray's winged armchair stood in its usual place, as if waiting for his return. There was fingerprint powder on the heavy brass fender in front of the fireplace, also on the window-catches, though there was no sign of a forced entry. The mysterious stranger who had met his death there had seemingly come in through the front door like any expected visitor. And, even if he had been an unexpected one, he had still been admitted.

Beyond an open archway in the far wall was a small room which Mr Gray used as a study. His old-fashioned roll-top desk with a functional modern swivel chair were the only bits of furniture. The desk-top was closed and locked. Rosa had no idea where he kept the key – not that she wished to make a detailed search. She found, too, that the lower drawers of the desk were also locked. It seemed likely that one master key unlocked the whole desk.

She walked back across the living room and out into the wide passage. Janet Berry's room lay next to the kitchen. Rosa pushed open the door and went in.

The bed was made and the room had a tidy look, as though its occupant's departure had been unhurried. And there was something else. The top of the dressing table was bare. Rosa recalled having noticed a hairbrush and bottles of hand lotion and skin moisturiser on previous occasions, as well as other customary aids to feminine beauty. She slid back the door of the built-in cupboard. A number of dresses still hung inside, but there were gaps to suggest that others had been removed. The drawers of the dressing table gave a similar impression.

Janet Berry might have had time to pack some of her things, but had seemingly been prevented from taking all her belongings.

Rosa stood in thought in the middle of the room as she pondered the implications. She was drawn to the conclusion that Janet Berry must have been involved in what had happened. Involved actively, that is. It no longer seemed likely, if it ever had, that she had been forcibly abducted. She returned to Mr Gray's bedroom and made a further investigation. By contrast his drawers and wardrobe were full of his clothes, though the small array of pill-bottles on his bedside table had gone. This seemed to indicate that he was expecting to live when he left – or that someone was expecting it on his behalf. She recalled that he had a bottle of

39

sleeping tablets, as well as pills for his blood-pressure and for occasional attacks of angina.

She wondered if the police were aware of this. If Mrs Henderson had noticed – and little escaped her observant eye – she would certainly have told them. She imagined they would also have drawn their own conclusions about Janet Berry's depleted wardrobe.

It was with a slight jolt that she realised that nothing she had discovered began to explain the presence of a dead stranger in Mr Gray's bed. And yet she felt that he must have been involved in something with Janet Berry; or at least must have been known to her. The fact that Mrs Berry had taken with her much more than Mr Gray seemed to refute any suggestion that they had been co-conspirators. In any event, conspirators in what? She had a mind's-eye picture of the two of them leaving, Mrs Berry carrying one or more bits of luggage while Mr Gray clutched his pill-bottles and nothing else.

She decided there was nothing further to be gained by remaining at the flat. Indeed, very little else to be done at all until one or other of them turned up. It seemed unlikely that Mr Gray and his housekeeper could disappear for ever in overpopulated Britain. Sooner or later there was bound to be news of them.

Locking the front door behind her, Rosa walked towards the lift. On the spur of the moment she suddenly changed direction and went over to Mrs Fox's door. There had been no sound of singing, which might mean she was out. But the door opened suddenly and Mrs Fox stood there, a vast purple figure.

'Hello, dear, you're Mr Gray's solicitor, aren't you? Would you like to come in? I was just about to have a cup of lime tea. Will you join me?'

'Thank you very much,' Rosa said as Mrs Fox moved aside to let her pass.

Rosa hadn't had lime tea since she had spent three months as a student with a French family in Versailles. It used to be served after each meal, and she had become quite addicted to its distinctive flavour. Now a decade later she was being offered it again.

She glanced round the room into which Mrs Fox had

40

shown her before disappearing into the kitchen, from where there now came a hummed snatch of *Carmen*.

A table next to the fireplace had about a dozen framed photographs on it, each showing Mrs Fox in one of her operatic roles. A well-upholstered Rhinemaiden in *Das Rheingold*, a peasant in *The Marriage of Figaro*, another peasant in *Otello* and, in pride of place, Carmen herself in an austerity post-war production somewhere in the north of England.

Rosa was still studying the photographs when Mrs Fox reappeared bearing a tray with a silver teapot and two delicate cups and saucers.

'Those are just a few of the roles I sang,' Mrs Fox remarked with a note of genuine pride. 'I was always prepared to sing in the chorus if the production was a good one. At Covent Garden, I've sung under Beecham and Kempe and Solti and all the great conductors of my time. Oh my, and couldn't some of them be difficult! But I never minded provided I could respect their musicianship.' She put the tray down on a low table. 'I hope you'll like lime tea.'

'I know I will,' Rosa said, and went on to relate her experience of it.

'That's where I first came across it, too,' Mrs Fox said in a delighted tone. 'I was studying singing in Paris under the legendary Madame Breuil. I don't suppose you've ever heard of her. It was long before your time. But Madame Breuil used to refresh herself with lime tea when she was giving a recital.'

Mrs Fox had perched herself on the forward edge of a sturdy chair in front of the tray and began pouring. The purple garment she was wearing became a single precipitous slope from her neckline to her feet.

'So what tidings do you bring of Mr Gray?' she enquired, rather as if greeting one of opera's ubiquitous messengers.

'There's no news of him at all. It's extremely puzzling, not to say worrying. I imagine the police have been to see you.'

'Yes, but there was little I could tell them. I've never sought to do more than remain on civil terms with my neighbours, though that hasn't always been easy. Mrs Henderson, for example, is an extremely domineering woman, and I'm afraid your Mr Gray didn't always show the manners of a gent-leman.'

'I take it you never heard any untoward sounds coming

from Mr Gray's flat over the weekend?'

'Such as dead bodies that go bump in the night?' she said
with a quizzically raised eyebrow. 'No, not a thing. This is a
solidly built block and as near soundproof as it could be.' It
was Rosa's turn to raise a quizzical eyebrow. 'Yes, I know that
Mr Gray and Mrs Henderson have complained about my
singing, but they just wanted to be difficult. Mrs Henderson
would back anything Mr Gray said. He was her tame good
cause – not that I think he encouraged her.' She paused and
stared down the purple slope that ended at her feet. 'As a
matter of fact I have recalled one detail since the police spoke
to me. It was Monday night late; I went to put an empty
milk-bottle outside my door and heard the click of Mr Gray's
front door being closed. I didn't think anything of it at the
time, and indeed it slipped completely from my mind until
now. Do you think I ought to tell the police?'

'I think you probably should,' Rosa replied. 'About what
time was this?'

'Just after midnight. The milkman comes early and I always
put the empty bottles out overnight.'

'You didn't hear anything further?'

'No – but I wouldn't have once I was in my bedroom.'

Rosa looked thoughtful. 'So it looks as if there was someone
in Mr Gray's flat as late as Monday night, and on Tuesday Mrs
Henderson returns and sets everything in motion. I wonder if
somebody returned to complete their unfinished business. I
gathered from the police that the body had been dead for
three or four days. That means since last Saturday or
Sunday.'

Mrs Fox nodded placidly. 'Poor man! Thank goodness I'm
not a particularly nervous person, though I don't mind telling
you, my dear, that I now double-lock my door at night. I'm
not having anyone slip a dead body into *my* bed.'

The possibility that the corpse might have been delivered
uninvited had not occurred to Rosa, and it didn't take her
long to dismiss it.

'How well do you know Mr Welling?' she asked after a
pause.

'Now there *is* a gentleman,' Mrs Fox declared. 'He may not
have been born one, but he has the instincts of a natural

gentleman. Believe me, my dear, I've known men of good breeding who behaved like pigs and others of humble birth who were nature's gents. Arthur Welling is one of those.'

Taken aback by the vigour of her remarks, Rosa merely nodded. She felt Mr Welling might have been equally surprised.

'Mr Welling would do anything for anyone,' Mrs Fox went on. 'He was the one who stuck up for me when Mr Gray and Mrs Henderson made a fuss about my singing. Of course, they're both complete philistines with no musical appreciation at all.' She gave a loud sniff. '"The Skater's Waltz" is about the limit of Mr Gray's knowledge of music.'

'Do you happen to know if Mr Welling and Mrs Berry saw much of one another?'

'I know he invited her to one of his clubs and that she used to go there from time to time. It was a typical act of kindness. He took pity on her being cooped up with that old man all day and suggested she might like to visit one of his places.'

'Have you ever been to one?' Rosa asked.

'Indeed, I have. He invited me to dinner at the Golden Sands Club and afterwards persuaded me to sing. We had a riotous evening.'

Somehow Rosa couldn't picture Mrs Fox and the Golden Sands Club having much affinity with one another.

'What sort of club is it?' she asked, curious.

'There's a very nice restaurant with a small bar at one end and then there's gambling in another part of the building. Everything's very tastefully done and above board. I assure you there's nothing sleazy about the Golden Sands Club,' she added emphatically.

'Are his other clubs the same?'

'I believe so, but I know the Golden Sands is regarded as the jewel in the crown. Though it's not really my cup of tea, I thoroughly enjoyed my evening. Mr Welling was a most generous and attentive host.'

'What are the names of his other clubs?'

'There's the Sea Urchin and the Green Leaf Club.'

'Does gambling go on there as well?'

'You'll have to ask him, my dear. If he ever told me, I've forgotten.' A dreamy look came into her eyes. 'They made a

43

nice pair, Mr Welling and Mr Gray's housekeeper. They were well suited.'

'What makes you say that?' Rosa said with a slight frown.

'I felt they'd both had unhappy experiences in the past with the opposite sex and were now ready to try again.'

A few minutes later Rosa got up to go. Her visit to Mongton might not have produced any startling revelations, but it had been far from fruitless.

'I have a back door,' Mrs Fox said with a glint in her eye. 'Would you like to go out that way? It'll save you running the gauntlet past Mrs Henderson's door.'

Rosa smiled. 'That's a good idea,' she said. 'Thanks for the thought.'

'It's really a fire exit out of my kitchen which leads on to the emergency staircase in the adjoining block. You can then take the lift down from there.'

Rosa followed her out of the room and a few minutes later was in the road which ran along the front of the block.

'I'll call a taxi to pick you up at the corner,' Mrs Fox had said conspiratorially as they parted company.

On her journey back to London, Rosa tried to assemble her thoughts on her client's mysterious disappearance. The core of the puzzle was the unidentified corpse in his bed. He mightn't prove to be the Man in the Moon as Sergeant York had speculated but, beyond that, everything about him was a total mystery.

CHAPTER 4

Each time her phone rang during the next few days, Rosa felt sure it must be with news of Mr Gray. She and Sergeant York had been exchanging calls regularly, always in the apparent hope that the other might have information about the missing couple.

But after eight days without news Rosa no longer expected that her client would be found alive. Common sense dictated that he must be presumed dead. He was an old man in frail health who was unlikely to have survived the ordeal of abduction, always assuming that he had not been deliberately killed. As for Mrs Berry, Rosa was more certain than ever that she must have been involved in some criminal activity. She couldn't believe that both of them were somebody else's innocent victims.

Seeing that it was she, Rosa, who had found Mrs Berry, it was an uncomfortable decision to reach. Admittedly, Mr Gray had endorsed her appointment, if somewhat grudgingly. But that was how it had been with all his housekeepers. He had always raised carping objections. One had worn too much make-up. Another had offended by wearing none at all. 'Looks like one of Dracula's victims,' Mr Gray had remarked.

None the less Rosa was left with a feeling of guilt, which Mrs Henderson's too frequent reminders that *she* had never liked or trusted Mrs Berry did nothing to diminish.

'There's absolutely nothing you can do, so stop fretting,' Robin said firmly whenever Rosa poured out her concern. 'The police have the matter in hand, and all you can do is wait. I agree it now seems unlikely Mr Gray will be found alive. Either his body will be discovered or Mrs Berry will surface somewhere. I think the former is likely to happen first.'

Rosa nodded unhappily and pushed back her hair, which had a habit of falling forward on either side of her face.

'It's awful to feel so impotent.'

'It's time you learnt not to chafe at things over which you have no control. It's a waste of energy. Your trouble is that you want to have every situation developing all the time. You're dangerously close to becoming a workaholic. You need to cultivate more outside interests.'

'I've got masses,' Rosa said defensively. 'I read, I go to the theatre and to concerts. I watch enough television to justify the licence fee. And I get asked out quite a lot. So what do you want me to take up now? Japanese flower-arranging? Ballroom dancing? Judo, so that I can fend off any more aggressive clients?'

Robin held up his hands in mock surrender. 'Perhaps yoga might be more to the point.'

Both of them were well aware that he had in fact been referring to Rosa's lack of a steady boyfriend. In Robin's view it was a terrible waste that somebody who was attractive and fun to be with didn't have a regular male in her life. It also worried him that she seemed susceptible only to the dubious charms of amoral young men, whom he deemed to be totally unsuitable. He winced when he recalled some of the short-term affairs she'd had with these predatory prototypes, though miraculously she seemed to emerge emotionally unscathed.

Rosa was well aware of what Robin and various friends felt about her love-life, but was serenely untouched by their concern. If she fell from time to time for one of the firm's importunate young clients, that was her business, as long as it didn't affect her work. She thought it was probably the sheer cheek of their assumptions, coupled with their faith in her ability to see them through to the other side of trouble, that attracted her to them.

It was while they were each silently pursuing their own thoughts on this sensitive topic that Robin's phone rang. He reached out for the receiver.

'Stephanie says Mrs Tresant is on the line and wants to speak to you.'

Rosa got up. 'Tell Steph I'll take the call in my own room.'

She hurried off, leaving Robin to return his mind to trying to understand the technicalities of a computer fraud which one of his clients had ingeniously perpetrated. Successfully, too, to the tune of half a million pounds....

'Rosa Epton speaking,' Rosa said as she picked up the phone on her desk.

'It's about Philip,' Jean Tresant said in a nervous gush. 'His doctor suggested I speak to you, Miss Epton. I'd be so grateful for your help.'

'What exactly's happened?' Rosa asked in a puzzled tone.

'He's been in bed for the past three days and refuses to get up. The doctor can't find anything wrong with him and puts it all down to this case that's hanging over him. He thinks Philip's refusing to face reality and is trying to run away from life. He's prescribed tranquillisers and some other tablets to reduce his anxiety, but so far to no effect. Philip just lies in bed asleep or staring into space when he's awake. It's as though he's in a state of self-induced shock.'

Jean Tresant was obviously distraught, and Rosa felt touched by the note of desperation in her voice.

'What exactly does the doctor think I can do?' she asked dubiously.

'He believes the court case should be dealt with as soon as possible. He says it's the waiting that's the basic cause of Philip's state of withdrawal. He thinks any undue delay can only aggravate his condition.'

'Has he talked to Philip to that effect?'

'Yes.'

'And?'

'It's difficult to know what's going through Philip's mind. He doesn't really react any longer. He just shakes or nods his head when I ask him whether he's hungry or thirsty and things of that sort. Otherwise he scarcely responds at all.'

'Surely a psychiatrist is the person to help him.'

'Dr Miller's been trained in psychiatry, though he's now a GP. He's certain his diagnosis is correct. He feels any postponement of Philip's trial could have disastrous effects on Philip's mental health.'

Her voice broke, and at the other end of the line Rosa shook her head in mute sympathy.

47

'So what precisely does Dr Miller think I can do to help?'

'Come and visit Philip and impress on him that the case is definitely going ahead on the day fixed and that he's got to pull himself together and come to court. I'm sure it would boost his morale if you could tell him he has a good chance of getting off.'

Rosa sighed. This all seemed much more the doctor's job than hers. Moreover, she was none too sanguine about his chances of an acquittal. There were too many imponderables: the composition of the court, the credibility of the main prosecution witness under pressure, and, not least, her own client's performance in the witness-box. Before she could reply, however, Jean Tresant went on.

'Philip has such confidence in you, Miss Epton. He really has. Please say you'll come and see him. It isn't just me being hysterical, it's what Dr Miller recommends.'

'When?' Rosa asked.

'As soon as possible. At the moment he's just lying there like a zombie. I've explained to his firm that he's ill and, of course, Dr Miller's given him a certificate that says he'll be off work for at least a week. But, if something doesn't happen soon, I'll have a breakdown myself.'

'I'll come this evening,' Rosa said with sudden decision. 'About six o'clock, all right?'

'Oh, I'm so grateful. I'll see you then.'

The Tresants lived in a large semi-detached house in a pleasant tree-lined road in the south-western suburbs where a number of old and new boroughs met.

Both upstairs and downstairs lights were on when Rosa pulled up outside. Though she had not been to the house before, she knew the area and had no difficulty finding it.

Jean Tresant opened the front door while Rosa was still closing the garden gate.

'Thank you for coming, Miss Epton,' she said as they shook hands. 'I can't tell you how relieved I am that you're here.'

'Does Philip know about my visit?'

She nodded. 'I said that, as he was unwell, you'd very kindly agreed to call and discuss a few outstanding details before next week's hearing. On Dr Miller's advice, I've not let him think there's any question of a postponement. Shall we go straight up?'

'There are one or two points I'd like to mention first.'

'Yes, of course, let's go into the living room.'

When they were seated, Rosa said: 'Should he be found guilty, I shall need to make a plea in mitigation – not that I would expect more than a fine to be imposed in any event. . . .'

Jean Tresant gave her a haggard look and burst out: 'Whatever the penalty, nothing can equal the disgrace. Stealing from the collection-plate in church. . .'

'Yes, I do realise that,' Rosa went on quickly, 'but it'll be important, in the event of his conviction, to call witnesses to character.' Rosa paused. She had never been sure to what extent Jean Tresant was aware of her husband's history of minor peculations, even if none of them had yet resulted in a court appearance. 'Can you suggest somebody?'

'I'm sure the rector would testify.'

'You don't think he'd prefer to remain aloof, seeing that it's two of his parishioners who are involved?'

'He's a friend of the family, Miss Epton. I know he'd speak up for Philip. And, if it doesn't sound too unchristian to say so, Mr Provis has never been a particularly well-liked member of our church. I don't know why he's chosen to persecute my husband in this spiteful way. I suppose every community has thorns in its flesh, and Gerald Provis is certainly one.'

Rosa couldn't help reflecting that there were probably those who regarded Philip Tresant in a similar light.

'Who else apart from the rector, if he'll come? What about one of the directors of his company?'

A frown settled on Jean Tresant's face.

'As you know he's only been with Hilmorton's for a year and he's never really settled there. In fact he's been looking around for another job.'

Rosa's understanding was that Hilmorton's was a thrusting young company in the holiday tours market, in which no one less than a fully fledged whiz-kid had much chance of surviving. She'd had the impression that Philip Tresant didn't fit in, even in the relative obscurity of the audit department. Jean Tresant's remark seemed to confirm all this.

'Well, don't worry now,' she said quickly. 'Why don't we go up and see your husband?'

'I suppose Philip's told you about the family business?' Jean Tresant said as they got up. Rosa shook her head. As a matter

49

of fact she had always found him extremely reticent about his family background, but hadn't been too concerned about this in view of the nature of the charge. If it had been murder, for instance, she would have felt obliged to probe more persistently. 'Then, I think it's something you should know,' Jean Tresant went on, 'though Philip and his brother have never liked talking about it and I don't even know all the details myself. Their father founded and ran a family business, but something happened and it went bust, just as James Tresant – that's Philip's father – was about to retire and hand over to Malcolm, who was his elder son. Shortly afterwards he committed suicide, and his wife, Philip's mother, died of a broken heart within twelve months. This all happened before I ever met Philip and, given his nature, I suppose it's not surprising he's never wanted to talk about it.'

'How long ago was this?'

'About ten years. I met Philip shortly after his mother's death and we were married almost immediately. So I never knew his parents. Sadder is the fact that the children have been deprived of grandparents on that side.'

'What about the brother?'

'Malcolm's never married. He's seven years older than Philip and lives in a small flat in north London. He's the artistic one. He designs things.'

'What sorts of thing?'

'Almost anything. Wallpaper, Christmas cards, decorative panels. He's really very talented, but he doesn't have particularly good health. We don't see him all that often. At least, I don't.' She paused and threw Rosa a quick look. 'In case you're wondering,' she said with a wry smile, 'my father bought this house for us. My parents are fairly affluent, and I'm their only child.' She turned as they were going out of the door. 'Philip's never told you any of this?'

'No.'

'Probably better, then, not to let on that I have.' She appeared to blink away an onset of tears. 'He's not just my husband and the father of my children, but I love him more than anyone in the world.'

They arrived upstairs and she paused before a door.

'Actually this is the spare bedroom,' she whispered over her shoulder. 'Philip's been so restless at nights, he said it'd be better if he slept on his own.' She turned the handle. 'Are you awake, darling? Miss Epton's here.'

Philip Tresant was lying on his back in one of the two single beds, staring up at the ceiling. He moved his head slightly as Rosa entered and his lips twitched in what she took to be a smile.

'I'll leave you two alone to talk,' his wife said with false cheerfulness as she went out, closing the door firmly behind her.

'How are you feeling?' Rosa asked, for want of any other way of starting things.

He shook his head vaguely as though it were too difficult a question to answer.

'You've got to be fit by next Tuesday,' she went on. 'That's the day we go to court. Your wife and the doctor both think it's vital you get the case over, and I'm sure they're right. They feel that any delay or postponement won't do your health any good.' She stared down at the prone listless figure and wondered why he wasn't able to stir any chord of sympathy in her. She marvelled that he'd been able to find such a loving, caring wife. 'I can't, of course, guarantee results,' she went on, 'but you have a very reasonable chance of being acquitted. As I've told you before, it'll be your word against Mr Provis's and everything will depend on the impression each of you makes in the witness-box. I'll do my best to dent his credibility, but it's important you come to court in a positive frame of mind. Confident, but not arrogantly so. You're entitled to rely on your good character, by which I mean the fact that you've never been in trouble with the law before, in particular for any offence involving dishonesty.' As she spoke, he stared at her dispassionately and without any indication of a raw nerve being touched. Not that she wanted him to break down and confess his kleptomaniac-al tendencies. Indeed, it was the very last thing she wished for. It would be a grave embarrassment to his advocate, whose role was to say everything on his behalf that he would say for himself. She wasn't there to put forward her own beliefs. 'I want you to promise me that you'll be in court next Tuesday. Dr Miller will supply you with the necessary medical

51

support, and your wife will give you all the emotional support you need. And I'll be there to man the legal bastions. So will you make up your mind that you'll be there? If you don't, it'll be that much worse later on, because nothing's going to make the case go away. Sooner or later you must face the ordeal, and the sooner the better for both you and your wife. She's told me how much she loves you and she's under as much strain as you are.'

He gave her a pale tired look. 'It's all right. I'll be there.'

'Good! Is there anything you want to ask me before I go?' He shook his head. 'We'll be able to have a chat in court on the morning of the case but, if anything occurs to you meanwhile, you can get in touch with me.'

'Thank you.'

'And start thinking positively,' Rosa said with a small smile as she reached the door. It was an admonition that evoked no response, however. His gaze that followed her out of the room was about as lustrous as grey flannel.

Jean Tresant emerged from the kitchen as Rosa came downstairs and looked at her hopefully.

'He's promised to be there next Tuesday.'

'Thank you for achieving that,' she said with a surge of obvious relief.

'He's clearly in a state of acute depression. Do you think there's anything else preying on his mind, apart from the case?'

'As I mentioned, he's not been happy at work for some while, but there's nothing else as far as I know. He's always been a mass of inhibitions.' She gave Rosa a forlorn smile. 'I don't suppose I'm the first wife to have failed to exorcise her husband's inhibitions. I used to believe that once we were married he would shed them like a snake shedding its skin, but I'm afraid that's never happened. It was probably naïve of me to think otherwise. Anyway, I'm so grateful to you for coming this evening.'

'Did he just refuse to get up one morning?' Rosa asked with a slight frown. 'Is that how it all began?'

'No, he came home last Friday evening looking utterly drained and exhausted. He said he wasn't feeling well and he went straight up to bed without eating his dinner. He's been

52

there ever since.' Her expression clouded. 'When I phoned his office on Monday morning and spoke to the personnel manager, I was told he hadn't been in on Friday and they'd wondered what had happened. It's obvious now that he must have spent the day wandering the streets in a state of shock.'

'Has he said as much?'

'No, and I've not asked him about it. Dr Miller advised against pressing him with questions. He said it could do more harm than good.'

There'd be no avoiding questions when they got to court, Rosa reflected grimly. She didn't know who would be conducting the prosecution, but questions would certainly be part of his armoury. So long as Philip Tresant protested his innocence, he was bound to go into the witness-box and face questions, first from Rosa and then from prosecuting counsel.

She had always foreseen that it was a case which could develop into a really dirty fight. And all over five pounds from the collection-plate. She presumed the Almighty had seen what had happened, but she was glad that He would refrain from showing His hand – at any rate, too obviously.

CHAPTER 5

ROSA HAD JUST arrived back in the office from court the next afternoon when Sergeant York phoned.

'We've had a sighting of a woman answering Mrs Berry's description,' he said without preliminary as soon as he was put through. 'An off-duty woman police officer spotted her in a supermarket in Birmingham. She was with a man of about her own age and they were in the process of selecting a pack of pork chops when the officer saw them. Unfortunately they must have become aware of her surveillance because while she was away alerting two officers on the pavement outside they vanished. The WPC was certain they'd exit by one of the cash-desks where she'd see them, but they didn't. A subsequent search showed that they'd abandoned their basket of purchases behind a pillar and had apparently slipped out by one of the emergency doors into a passage at the side of the building.'

'Obviously it was somebody with a bad conscience, even if it wasn't Mrs Berry,' Rosa observed.

'Oh, I think it was her all right. I've spoken to the WPC myself, and she sounded a pretty bright sort of girl.'

'I gather there was nobody answering Mr Gray's description with them?'

'You'd hardly expect them to have taken him shopping, would you, Miss Epton?'

'No, not really. I wonder how many pork chops they bought.'

'I can tell you. It was a pack of two. Not that that proves anything, either way.'

'So what's the next move?' Rosa asked after a pause.

'The police in the area will be on further look-out for the

couple, though I suspect they will either lie low for a time or have already slipped away. Do you know whether Mrs Berry had any connection with Birmingham?'

'Not that I recall. She'd been working in London before Mr Gray engaged her, and I seem to remember her saying she'd been born and brought up in Southampton.'

Sergeant York sighed. 'Birmingham's as good a place as anywhere to hide in. A great sprawling city in the centre of the country, just made for anonymous living.'

'All we can do is hope the trail can be kept alive,' Rosa said. 'Meanwhile, thanks for letting me know.'

'You don't have anything new to tell me?'

'Not a thing. I'll probably come down to Mongton tomorrow. I ought to go through Mr Gray's mail and see whether there's anything requiring urgent attention.'

'There's not,' Sergeant York said without hesitation. 'We've been keeping an eye on it for possible clues as to his whereabouts.'

Rosa was about to protest, then quickly recalled that her client wasn't a mere missing person, but one who had left a dead body behind in his bed.

She had it in mind to call on Dr Nagy, also to try to talk to Arthur Welling. Definitely absent from her agenda would be any meeting with Mrs Henderson. Shortly after Sergeant York had rung off she put through a call to Dr Nagy's surgery. A cool-voiced receptionist answered and briskly enquired what was wrong with her before Rosa had time to explain why she wanted to see the doctor.

'There's nothing wrong with me, but I wish to talk to Dr Nagy about a client of mine who is also his patient. Mr Vernon Gray of Southview Court. I imagine Dr Nagy knows that he has disappeared in somewhat mysterious circumstances.'

If he did, his receptionist wasn't saying.

'Hold on and I'll find out if Dr Nagy can see you,' she said coldly.

Though Mr Gray had told Rosa that he had asked his doctor to be an executor of his will, she was by no means sure that he had done so. He had been testily offhand when she pressed him on the subject. It was something she must try to find out when she met Dr Nagy.

The cool voice broke in on her thoughts. 'Dr Nagy suggests you come around half-past ten. He should have finished his morning surgery by then and be free to see you. If you have to cancel the appointment, please let me know immediately.'

'Of course, but I shan't,' Rosa retorted, and rang off while the last word remained hers.

A call to Mr Welling's number produced no answer. She would now wait until she reached Mongton to call him.

At ten twenty-five the next morning she presented herself at Dr Nagy's surgery, which turned out to be the ground floor of a large detached house. From the labelling beside the bells, it appeared that somebody lived in the upper floors and that the ground floor was used for professional purposes. From the nameplate at the side of the door, Dr Nagy appeared to be the senior of three partners.

A thin-faced woman with a discontented mouth and an elaborate mauve hair-do was busy writing when Rosa reached reception. Eventually, however, she looked up and slid back the glass panel between them.

'Yes?' she said in an unwelcoming tone.

'I'm Rosa Epton. I have an appointment with Dr Nagy. I phoned yesterday from London.'

The woman frowned as though a mosquito had disturbed her peace. 'Oh, yes, I think I remember. Take a seat in the waiting room. When you hear the buzzer, go to the room on the right at the end of the corridor. It has Dr Nagy's name on the door.' She closed the glass panel to indicate that communication was over.

I wonder what our Stephanie would think of her, Rosa reflected as she turned to go into the waiting room. Not that Stephanie couldn't put a client in his place, though usually with good reason.

An old man was wheezing in one corner of the waiting room, which was otherwise empty.

'It's my chest,' he said, giving Rosa an unmistakable leer. 'Doctor says he's never seen one like it. Real chronic it is. He doesn't know how I keep going, but I tells him it's the only one I've got. I was a prisoner during the last war, you see.

56

Joined up when I didn't need to. Could have had a cushy job back home, but I went off with the lads and got captured in 1940. How old would you say I was now?'

Fortunately, at that moment a bell gave a shrill *ping* and the old man got up. 'That's for me,' he said with a final rheumy leer as he shuffled past Rosa, wheezing like a pair of ancient bellows.

She wondered whether many of Snaith & Epton's clients were waiting-room bores. Probably not, she thought. Tales of chronic chests and infected bladders and other intestinal goings-on produced a special sort of camaraderie.

She had hardly picked up a six-month-old copy of *Vogue* when the buzzer summoned her.

'I'm so sorry to have kept you waiting, Miss Epton,' Dr Nagy said, getting up from behind his desk as she entered. 'I had to dictate an urgent letter to the hospital about one of my patients. Please sit down and make yourself comfortable.'

He was a small man with a quick lively expression. He had black springy hair flecked with grey and a smooth face that wouldn't have kept a razor-blade factory in business.

'So you want to talk about Mr Gray,' he went on, as though it were a moment he'd been eagerly awaiting.

'I suppose you know that he and his housekeeper have disappeared?'

'How could I not know? The police have been to see me.'

'Ah! Were you able to give them any help?'

'Only by telling them the medicaments I've prescribed from time to time.' He spoke almost flawless English with only a slight accent, but now said: 'You must excuse me if I sometimes use a wrong word. Even after thirty years here, my English isn't perfect.'

'It sounds perfect to me.'

'You should see my spelling,' he said with a chuckle. 'My children think I'm a barbaric foreigner. Not all the time, you understand; only when I'm cross with them. It's then they retaliate by telling me I can't speak English. But let us go back to Mr Gray.'

'May I ask you whether he ever said anything to you about making a will?'

Dr Nagy looked uncertain and discomforted.

57

'He asked me if I would be an executor of his will. It was only a short time ago. He said he was making a new will as his previous executors had died. He told me you were his solicitor and would attend to all the legal details on his death.'

From what he had just said, Rosa deduced that Mr Gray hadn't asked him to be an executor until well after the will had been made. As for saying that the executors of his previous will had died, Rosa accepted that as a piece of harmless deception. Nevertheless, when she later went along to the flat she would make sure there wasn't an earlier will hidden anywhere. She had come armed with a bunch of desk-keys, lent to her by a one-time client who had specialised in opening other people's drawers and who had sworn by his dear mother's memory that one of the bunch would open Mr Gray's desk.

'Did he tell you anything about the contents of his will?' Rosa now asked.

Dr Nagy looked shocked. 'I didn't wish to hear anything about it. He did say I could expect a small legacy, but I told him not to tell me more.' He gave Rosa a disarming smile. 'It is not unknown for patients to make bequests to their doctors, but it is not something I would encourage.'

Rosa knew nothing about how such matters were regarded in Hungary, but could think of at least one notorious English doctor who had become rich under the terms of his grateful patients' wills. At all events it was apparent that Dr Nagy was wholly unaware he was the principal beneficiary under Mr Gray's will.

'Was Mrs Berry also your patient?' she asked.

'She was registered with me, but she was never ill. I saw her only once. Professionally, that is.' He paused. 'In view of what has happened, I tell you about it in confidence. She thought she might be going to have a baby.'

'Good gracious! Surely Mr Gray couldn't have been the putative father?'

'Tests showed that she wasn't pregnant.'

'How soon was this after she became his housekeeper?'

'It was about two months ago, and she was very agitated at the possibility of having a child. I had the impression she didn't want a particular person to find out.'

58

'You've no idea who that person was?'

'None. None whatsoever. It is better that way, yes?'

'That could depend,' Rosa remarked thoughtfully.

His phone rang, and she took the opportunity of studying him covertly while he answered it. She wondered what his reaction would be if she were to apprise him of the contents of Mr Gray's will. It mightn't be long before he learnt anyway.

When he had finished speaking on the phone, Rosa got up to leave. He accompanied her to the door and they shook hands.

'I am glad to have met you, Miss Epton. Let us hope nothing bad has happened to Mr Gray, though I fear his age and general health are against him.'

'I have small hope of his being found alive.'

'You are probably right. I think he is probably deceased.'

'The question will be whether he has died naturally or violently by somebody's hand.'

'A violent death can often be a less painful death,' Dr Nagy observed philosophically.

The receptionist was still busy writing and didn't look up as Rosa departed. Her manner was in stark contrast with that of the doctor, and Rosa could only assume she had undisclosed merits.

She found a telephone-kiosk about a hundred yards down the road and decided to call Mr Welling. To her surprise he answered almost at once. After she had introduced herself and said she would like an opportunity of talking to him, his response was immediate.

'I'm just about to leave for my office where I have lunch most days. If you'd like a smoked-salmon sandwich and a glass of wine, why don't you join me there in about half an hour? It's the Golden Sands Club.'

'Thank you. I'd like to do that.'

'Splendid. No further news of Mr Gray, I suppose.'

'I'm afraid not.'

'Extraordinary business,' he murmured. 'See you shortly, Miss Epton.'

The main door of the Golden Sands Club was firmly closed when Rosa arrived. It looked as solid as a bank's and able to withstand a stampede of elephants or angry gamblers. She

59

pushed a bell and waited. After a pause, the door opened a fraction and a young man's face peered out.

'Mr Welling's expecting me,' she said.

'Then, you must be Miss Epton.' He pulled the door further open, and Rosa entered. 'My name's Chris and I'm the barman. I've come in to do a bit of clearing up. We don't open till six today. Actually, there's a private entrance at the side, but perhaps Mr Welling didn't tell you.'

'No, he didn't.'

'No harm done. But watch your step, Miss Epton. It's a bit like an obstacle course, not to say dingy, without all the lights on.'

Rosa followed him, stepping over cables and round upturned tables and chairs.

'Come back at six and you won't recognise the place,' Chris said cheerfully. 'At the moment it's like a stage before the scene's been set. I should know. I'm really an actor. Being a barman is simply a way of earning money. Not that I'm complaining. It's good fun in many ways, and you certainly meet different types in a place like this.'

While he'd been talking, they had ascended a short staircase that had a door at either end. As he opened the door at the top he stood aside to let Rosa pass. There was a small, thickly carpeted landing with three doors, each of which was marked 'Private'. He knocked on one of them.

'Miss Epton's here, Mr Welling,' he said, opening it.

'Thanks, Chris. Show her in.'

Rosa found herself ushered into an opulently equipped office that made her own, even with its new carpet, seem the poorest of poor relations. She reckoned Arthur Welling's desk alone must have cost several thousand pounds.

'Do sit down, Miss Epton. The food will be here in a minute. Meanwhile, let me pour you a glass of wine. That is, unless you'd sooner have something with more kick in it.'

'I'd prefer wine,' Rosa said. 'I don't normally drink at all in the middle of the day.'

'It's a good rule,' he observed, going across to a gold-plated trolley on which stood an array of bottles and glasses and an ice-bucket.

While he was pouring the wine, Rosa further examined her

surroundings. On three of the walls there were beachscape pictures with vistas of golden sand. Their overall effect was tasteless and unsubtle, though each in its own way was quite attractive.

He returned with the wine, and a moment later there was a knock on the door and Chris entered bearing a plate of delicately garnished sandwiches.

'Put them down on the desk between us, Chris,' Mr Welling said. 'Then let it be known I don't wish to be disturbed.'

'Will do, Mr Welling,' Chris said and departed.

'I don't want to waste your time,' Rosa said, 'but I would like to ask you one or two questions about Mr Gray's disappearance.'

'Certainly. It's a most extraordinary affair, isn't it?'

Brushing aside the comment, Rosa went on: 'I understand you knew Mrs Berry quite well.'

'I knew her, yes, She came here on a number of occasions. It was her only chance of a bit of recreation.'

'Was she accompanied by anyone?'

'Not as far as I'm aware. But as I don't stand guard at the entrance I wouldn't know.' His tone had become suddenly less friendly.

'Do you know whether she met people here ?'

'I would hope so. It would have been one of the reasons for coming. To get out and have a bit of company.'

'Do you recall any particular person she met here?'

'What are you getting at, Miss Epton?'

His voice conveyed a sudden note of menace, and Rosa leant forward to help herself to another sandwich to steady her resolve.

'I believe the police showed you a photograph of the dead man found in Mr Gray's bed?'

'They did, and I told them I'd never seen him before.'

'Was that true?'

For several seconds he stared at her in silence, and it was not a friendly look. She wondered if Mrs Fox would still proclaim him one of nature's gentlemen, were she to see him now.

'That strikes me as an offensive question,' he said, his face stiff with anger. 'In the circumstances, I have nothing further to say to you.' He paused a moment and went on: 'Except this. Should you be thinking of questioning my staff, you'll be wasting your time. They know nothing and have absolutely nothing to tell you.'

He pushed back his chair and rose, giving Rosa no choice but to do the same. He led the way out of the room and down the stairs. It was clear she was to have no opportunity of speaking to anyone on her way out. Chris was polishing glasses behind the bar as they passed. He gave her a smile, which quickly died when he observed his employer's expression.

So Arthur Welling obviously had recognised the dead man, Rosa reflected as she walked away from the Golden Sands Club. It was therefore a reasonable inference that he knew more about Mr Gray's disappearance than he was prepared to admit. Moreover, there was now a more obvious bond than ever between him and Janet Berry. Rosa's guess was that she and the dead man had met at the club, though even if they had it didn't help to solve the question of his identity, less still why he had ended up dead in Mr Gray's bed.

When Rosa arrived at Southview Court she took the lift to the fifth floor and walked up the final flight of stairs to the sixth. She hoped this would enable her to sneak into Mr Gray's flat without her arrival being monitored by Mrs Henderson. She wasn't to know that it was an unnecessary precaution as Mrs Henderson was at a church bazaar and Mrs Fox, too, was out, being lunched by a young man from a record company who was considering whether to reissue one of her very few recordings in their 'Golden Voices' series.

Mr Gray's flat already had a musty unoccupied smell, which assailed Rosa's nose as soon as she opened the front door. She went straight to the small study off the living-room where his desk was. The person who had lent her the keys had impressed on her that perseverance would be necessary to open it.

'It's like everything else,' he had said with a wink. 'If it's worth doing, you have to work at it. Don't expect the drawers to fly open with the first turn of the first key.'

And so it proved to be. But eventually one of the keys slid snugly into the lock and Rosa was able to turn it without undue force.

The first drawer she looked into contained bank statements and chequebook stubs. His most recent statement showed a current-account balance of over £3,000. He also had £82,000 on deposit. There was no doubt about his financial standing. There was no sign of a chequebook, and Rosa assumed it had gone at the same time as he had. She decided she ought to phone his bank and tell them to be cautious about clearing any cheques. It seemed possible that somebody else might be using them. At the bottom of the same drawer she found a single statement of account with the Piccadilly branch of one of the large banks. It was in the name of William Corley and showed a credit of £125,480 on a date in March 1978 and a withdrawal of the same amount at the beginning of April of the same year. Who was William Corley, if not Vernon Gray himself? More pertinent, perhaps, was why such a large sum had moved in and out of his account in such a short space of time all those years ago.

Rosa was well aware that people opened bank accounts in false names for reasons both sound and dubious and that banks were not renowned for taking moral stances where their own profit was concerned.

Putting everything back as she had found it, she opened the next drawer down. A glance told her it was the sort of drawer found in everyone's home. One in which anything was put which didn't have an obvious place elsewhere. It was overflowing with a miscellany of items. She picked up a Christmas card that had fallen to the floor. 'To G.,' it read, 'from J. and H.' Beneath was the year 1975. It was a pretty card, which can have been the only reason for keeping it all that time. She wondered who J. and H. were and why they addressed Mr Gray by his surname initial.

It was while she was burrowing deeper into the drawer that further items spilled out. She picked them up and found herself looking at a snapshot. It was of a man and woman and two boys aged about twelve and six. The man, who was tall and thin, was wearing a panama hat and smoking a pipe. His face was a blur, the photographer having obviously failed to focus the camera. In addition, it appeared that they were looking into a bright sun, for the boys' features were screwed up and their eyes were scarcely visible. The woman was wearing a wide-brimmed hat and a floral dress that hung loosely from her shoulders like a shift. She was the only one who might have been essaying a smile. The two boys had on shorts and open-necked shirts. Rosa reckoned the snapshot was all of twenty-five years old.

She peered more closely at the man and decided that it could be Mr Gray. He was of the same height and build, and the fact that she had never seen him smoke a pipe meant nothing in the circumstances. It was clearly a picture of a family on holiday, which meant that, if her assumption was correct, Mr Gray had had a wife and two sons. This was reinforced by a hazy familiarity about the younger boy's face. She felt she could detect a likeness with his father. On the back of the snapshot was pencilled 'Exmouth 1960'.

She wished Mr Gray's features were more recognisable, but the clue to his identity lay in the screwed-up face of the younger boy.

She returned the snapshot to the drawer and, after finding nothing further of interest, closed it.

She had spent longer than she'd intended and was ready to leave. She glanced quickly through the mail she had picked up from the floor on her arrival. There appeared to be nothing of any urgency. What might, or might not, be significant was the fact that there were no letters addressed to Mrs Berry.

Rosa felt her visit had produced results, even if she couldn't yet fully assess them.

CHAPTER 6

'MISS EPTON? It's Sergeant York. We've found Mr Gray. At least, it's someone who answers his description. He's dead, I'm afraid. I'd be glad if you could identify the body.'

It was three days since her visit to Mongton, and Rosa had begun to feel ever more dominated by Mr Gray's disappearance and its opaque circumstances.

'How did he die?' she asked.

'Drowned. His body was fished out of the Severn at Worcester.'

'Worcester?' Rosa echoed in surprise.

'Your geography's probably better than mine, Miss Epton, so you'll know it's not that far from Birmingham. Twenty-nine miles to be exact. I've checked.'

Rosa was thoughtful for a moment. 'So you think he and Mrs Berry were still together until he met his death?'

'Doesn't it strike you that way, too?'

'It's a possible inference,' Rosa said cautiously. 'How did he get in the river?'

'We don't yet know. I gather there are no external marks on the body, but there won't be a post-morten until later today. His body was caught up in the overhanging branches of a tree. A chap fishing on the opposite bank spotted it.'

'And you're reasonably sure it's my client?'

'All I can tell you is that it answers the description we put out. There were no identifying documents on the body. The local police got in touch with us and said they'd like a positive identification as soon as possible. Could you go down this afternoon? I can give you the train times from Paddington, and an officer will meet you at the station. You'll be back in London well before bedtime.' Sergeant York's voice held a note of pleading.

'I hope it's not a wild-goose chase,' Rosa said after a pause.

'I'm sure you agree it's in both our interests to have the matter cleared up,' he remarked with an obvious note of relief.

It was her awareness of this that prompted her decision to go. If anything, it was more in her interest than in anyone else's. At the moment, Mr Gray's affairs were in a state of suspended animation with Rosa coping uncertainly from day to day.

She glanced at her watch. If she left the office within the next fifteen minutes, she'd be able to catch the suggested train. Filling her briefcase with papers to read on the journey, she departed for the station, informing Stephanie where she was going on her way out.

It was around six o'clock when she arrived in Worcester. As she walked along the platform she observed a young police constable chatting animatedly to the ticket-collector at the barrier. He was wearing a flat cap, rather than a helmet, which indicated to her that he was a driver. As she approached, he gave her a swift appraising look, followed by a broad smile.

'Miss Epton? I'm PC Kettle. The car's just outside. First stop the mortuary, I gather. Had a good journey?'

He continued to prattle cheerfully as they made their way out of the station. By the time they reached the car, Rosa already knew that he'd been born in London, but had moved to Worcester to marry a girl in that city. That he had been in the police four years, that his mother had taken off with a Canadian after his father had been killed in an accident while working on the railways, and that this had happened when he, PC Kettle, was only five. Thereafter he had been brought up by his grandmother, who still lived in Bermondsey.

Rosa had the feeling of being force-fed with cocktail snacks as he continued telling her details of his life.

'Once a Londoner, always a Londoner, they say. But not in my case. I wouldn't go back for anything. You can't beat the country, and we have almost as much crime as you do up there. Drugs, murders, burglaries. Being a country copper these days is more than arresting the occasional poacher and stopping yokels for riding their bikes without lights.'

'I imagine the so-called yokels all drive cars these days,' Rosa observed.

'I'll say. Some pretty fancy ones at that. I gather the old boy you've come to have a look at slipped in the river and drowned.'

'Is that the pathologist's verdict?'

He nodded as he swung the car out to avoid a dog. 'I spoke to the mortuary attendant just before I came to the station. I rang to make sure he'd still be there when we arrived. He grumbled a fair bit. Had the nerve to say his supper would be getting cold. I told him beer was meant to be cold.'

Rosa caught a glimpse of the tower of the cathedral down a narrow street. She recalled having attended the Three Choirs Festival there as a teenager when her father was a country parson in neighbouring Herefordshire.

The car came to a sudden halt, and he jumped out and came round to open Rosa's door.

They were admitted to the mortuary by a man whose expression seemed to match his surroundings. He gave Rosa a brief nod but studiously ignored PC Kettle.

'This needn't take long,' he said pointedly. 'He's in that middle drawer.'

Rosa followed him across the room to where one wall was lined with what resembled large filing cabinets. The attendant pulled out one of the drawers and turned back the top of the sheet which covered the body.

Rosa found herself gazing into the face of a complete stranger. He might bear a superficial likeness to Mr Gray, but that was all.

'No, that's not my client,' she announced.

'All this hanging around for nothing,' the attendant said crossly.

'You're quite sure?' PC Kettle asked in a crestfallen tone.

'Absolutely sure.'

'I'll lock up, then,' the attendant said, sliding the drawer quickly back and heading towards the exit. Almost before Rosa and the officer had moved, he had begun switching off lights.

'I take it you'll phone Sergeant York and tell him the news?' Rosa said as they got back into the car.

'I'll have to. I felt certain it was going to be your client,' he remarked in a tone that seemed to imply that Rosa had let him down.

'Think of the fun you'll now have finding out who it really is,' she said brutally.

He gave her a hurt look, but she was in no mood to relent.

On the journey home, however, she came to feel that it had not been a complete wild-goose chase. Indeed, it had served a purpose, for she was now convinced that Mr Gray would eventually be found somewhere much closer to his home.

She no longer considered it realistic that he was being taken around the country like a piece of baggage.

CHAPTER 7

THE WEEKEND PASSED without further incident. Rosa phoned Sergeant York from home on Saturday morning and told him what he already knew. He sounded fed up and muttered darkly about unidentified bodies lying about in mortuaries, as though it were a national problem.

'Somebody must know who the man found in your client's bed is!' he said querulously.

Rosa refrained from reminding him that Arthur Welling might be one of them. After all, it was Sergeant York himself who had voiced his suspicion that the club-owner knew more than he was prepared to admit.

She spent the rest of Saturday morning giving her flat a thorough clean, while the washing machine got on with its work. In the afternoon she did some household shopping and finished the day by being taken out to dinner by Peter Chen. Peter was a solicitor of Chinese parentage whom she had met in connection with one of her cases.

They usually dined at an up-market Chinese restaurant of his selection where she would happily leave the choice of food to him, knowing that they would have an exquisite meal. He was an excellent companion, and Rosa always looked forward to their evenings out together. He was agreeably unconventional and as unstuffy as Rosa liked to think herself. They would converse about everything under the sun, but never too deeply about the law.

He normally picked Rosa up in his BMW, but on this occasion had asked if she would meet him at the restaurant as he had a business appointment in the area which would keep him late. Their venue this time was Hampstead, and Rosa took a taxi, arriving at the restaurant at precisely the same moment as he was parking his car.

'You look stunning,' he exclaimed as he embraced her on the pavement after insisting on paying off her taxi.

He was the only man she knew who could make a kiss on the cheek a distinctly sensual experience.

'Tell me what you've been up to to make you look so lovely,' he said when they were seated at their table and awaiting the drinks he had ordered

'Having a bath and putting on my Saturday-evening face,' Rosa said with a laugh.

'I'm sure you looked just as delectable in the mortuary,' Peter then replied. They had spoken on the phone earlier in the day, and she had mentioned her visit to Worcester.

'You're in uncommonly good spirits,' Rosa remarked.

'It's seeing you.' He gave her a beaming smile, which had more than a hint of suppressed excitement in it. 'As a matter of fact, I've just pulled off a deal on behalf of a client which has netted him two and a quarter million dollars.'

'I hope he was pleased.'

'Nothing like as pleased as I am. He's a wealthy Arab, and it takes more than two and a quarter million dollars to quicken his pulse rate.'

'And there am I dashing about after a missing client and getting ready to defend someone who's charged with stealing five pounds from the collection-plate in church.'

'Yours is the emotionally rewarding work,' Peter Chen said gravely.

'Hypocrite!'

He grinned, revealing small, very white teeth. I wonder if he'll ever look older than a sixth-former, Rosa reflected as she gazed back at him over the top of her glass.

'No, it's true,' he said. 'Criminal work is much more interesting than property deals and the like. Trouble is that one can't make a proper living out of defending criminals.'

'When did you ever need to make a living out of the law? You've often told me how you pick and choose your cases and work only when you feel like it.'

'That's only half-true.'

'What's the other half?'

70

'That I had to work hard to build up the sort of practice I have, which enables me now to pick and choose. Something I'm very good at.' He paused and beamed Rosa another boyish grin. 'But tell me about your missing client.'

'He's still missing and that's about all there is to say.'

'And the body in his bed?'

'Still unidentified.'

Peter Chen frowned. 'The answer obviously lies in Mr Gray's past. That's where you'll find the solution to everything.'

'I know very little about his past. He never talked about it.'

'All the more reason for probing it.'

Rosa told him of the photograph she had found in his desk drawer.

'That shows I'm right,' Peter said. 'You must scour his family background.'

'That's more easily said than done. And, anyway, until I know his fate, I have no authority to act like that. Supposing he turns up alive and finds I've been unearthing his past, he'd have every right to be furious. He'd probably have me struck off the roll.'

Peter Chen gave her a pitying look. 'You're just making excuses. You know that he'll no more turn up alive than the Emperor of China will.'

'I may suspect he's dead, but I don't know,' Rosa said defensively. 'I've already done more than was strictly within my remit.'

Peter Chen gave a graphic shrug. 'It's up to you. I'm just saying what I'd do if he were my client.'

'What about his neighbours?' Rosa asked, wishing to shift her ground. 'Do you think they could be involved?'

'Colourful but irrelevant,' Peter said in a dismissive tone.

'I'm not so sure that Arthur Welling's an irrelevance.'

'Perhaps not. From what you've told me previously, he would appear to know something not good for his health.' He paused, and his expression brightened. 'I owe you lots of good turns, Rosa, so why don't I visit the Golden Sands Club and see what I can find out? A Chinese person at a roulette table is as unobvious as a parson in a church. You know what

71

a race of gamblers we are. I'll go one day next week. Leave it to me! Meanwhile let me concentrate on what we're going to eat. I hope you're hungry, because I have exotic thoughts tonight.'

Rosa threw him a quizzical look, but his attention seemed to be focused entirely on the menu.

She let out a quiet sigh. She felt relaxed for the first time in several days.

CHAPTER 8

Rosa left it to the last moment on Monday afternoon to phone the Tresant home and make sure that Philip would be at court the next day. Jean Tresant answered.

'The doctor's been to see Philip this morning,' she said as soon as she recognised Rosa's voice. 'He's been getting up, but he still refuses to leave the house. I'm just praying that once the case is over he'll pull himself together. Dr Miller is still sure there's nothing physically wrong with him and that it's all in his mind. If he's no better in a few days' time, the doctor says he'll arrange for Philip to be admitted to hospital for a thorough examination. But I'm sure there'll be a marked improvement once tomorrow is over. I feel that even if the case goes against him he'll be on the mend once his ordeal is lifted.'

'Let's hope everyone is right about that,' Rosa said. 'Tell him I'll be in court early and we'll have a talk before we get going. Meanwhile I'll phone the clerk of the court and tell him we'll be ready.'

Rosa had already been in touch with the court to ensure there wouldn't be anybody on the bench who was personally acquainted with Philip Tresant. In view of his community activities she imagined that quite a number of the panel of magistrates probably knew him.

'I'm glad to hear you'll be ready, Miss Epton,' the clerk said when she got through. 'I've had quite a game finding an impartial bench, but I hope I've managed it. The chairman is a Roman Catholic from a neighbouring parish, and the two justices who will be sitting with him are respectively an atheist who eschews all church activities and a Mrs Renshaw who's only recently arrived in the area and been transferred to our panel from the one where she previously lived. She assures me she's never heard of Mr Tresant.'

'I'm sorry you've had so much bother,' Rosa remarked.

'It's all part of the day's work,' the clerk observed equably. 'We certainly want to avoid suggestions of bias from any quarter.'

'Who's prosecuting?' Rosa asked.

'Mr Tidman. He's a local solicitor who does a lot of work for the police. Ever met him?'

'No, I don't think I have.'

The clerk chuckled. 'He can be a bit of a firecracker.'

'I'll bring a bucket of water with me. Thanks for warning me.'

The magistrates' court was a new building put up to relieve pressure in an overworked jurisdictional area. Its façade resembled a small version of a 1930s cinema and it had already begun to show much the same signs of wear and tear.

The vestibule was almost empty when Rosa entered, but she immediately espied Philip Tresant sitting over in a corner with his wife. Putting on a determined smile, she walked over to them.

Philip Tresant looked up as she approached, and she was again shocked by his appearance. He looked drawn and dull-eyed. He had never had a great deal of colour in his cheeks, which were now the unhealthy shade of unbaked pastry. To make matters worse, he had an unsightly pimple on the side of his chin. His hair was slicked down in front, but tufts stuck out at the back. Rosa thought his wife had probably attempted to make him look tidy, rather like a mother before taking her small son to a party.

They both stood up, and Rosa saw that he was wearing a dark suit with a sober shirt and tie. At least he was appropriately dressed for the occasion.

'How are you feeling today?' she enquired cheerfully.

'All right,' he said without conviction, though he did give her a wisp of a smile.

'Is there anything you want to ask me before the case comes on? Anything at all?'

He shook his head as though indifferent to his fate.

'How long do you think it'll last, Miss Epton?' his wife enquired.

74

'I wouldn't have thought more than an hour and a half,' Rosa said. 'The facts fall within a very small compass, and you and Mr Provis are virtually the only witnesses. There'll be police evidence as to the service of the summons on you, and that's about it. Incidentally, the first thing that'll happen is that the clerk will read out the charge and tell you that you have the right to elect trial by jury at a crown court, but that the justices here can try you if you consent, to which you answer that you accept summary trial by this court. You'll then be asked to plead to the charge and you say "Not guilty". After that you'll have nothing further to do, apart from listen, until you go into the witness-box and give evidence. I shall ask if you can sit close to me so that you can give me whispered comments as the case proceeds. Particularly when Mr Provis is giving his evidence.'

'That's him just come in,' Jean Tresant said nervously.

Rosa turned her head and saw a tall white-haired man peering severely about him. He looked dressed for a funeral, which was perhaps what he felt he had come to attend. As she watched him he removed his spectacles and polished the lenses with a clean white handkerchief. Then, putting them back on, he stared about him with renewed severity.

'Do you know Mr Tidman, the prosecuting solicitor?' Rosa asked, turning back to her client.

He shook his head.

'Is he quite nice?' Jean Tresant said anxiously.

'He's certainly nobody to be afraid of,' Rosa replied. 'I've never met him, but I gather he does quite a lot of work at this court. I thought you might have heard of him.'

'We know Mr Parsons and Mr Oakley, who are solicitors in the area, but, as you know, Philip didn't wish to go to one of the local ones about his case. I'm sure he's told you how he saw your name in the newspaper that somebody left on the seat beside him in the Tube. That's right, isn't it, darling?' she went on a trifle breathlessly like an over-eager guest at a cocktail party.

Her husband nodded, while Rosa silently cursed people who left newspapers in trains.

'How lucky we are that chance led him to your door, Miss Epton!' Jean Tresant added.

Rosa managed a pleasant smile, even though it wasn't

exactly her own sentiment.'

After a further ten minutes during which she did her best to instil some confidence in her client, she suggested they should go and sit in court. It wouldn't be long, she said, before the case was called on and it would allow him time to get the feel of the courtroom.

The clerk gave her a friendly nod as she sat down in the lawyers' row and whispered that the prosecuting solicitor hadn't yet arrived. Rosa took her papers out of her briefcase and then sat back to study the three magistrates on the bench.

The chairman wore the patient impassive air of one used to listening and not showing his emotions. He was a man in his fifties, bald on top but with a surrounding fringe of honey-coloured hair. Mrs Renshaw on his left looked like a harassed housewife who had forgotten her shopping list. She kept on opening her handbag, peering in and then closing it again. The third member of the bench, who sat on the chairman's right and was presumably the atheist, wore an aloof expression.

There was a sudden eruption of sound at the back of the court as someone came bustling through the swing-doors.

'Mr Tidman's arrived,' the clerk whispered in Rosa's direction.

Rosa turned her head to see a small man, not much older than herself, take his place at the far end of the row in which she was sitting. He had a plump fresh-complexioned face and was wearing a stiff white collar several sizes too small so that his neck and cheeks looked as if they were about to burst their banks.

No wonder he's a firecracker, Rosa thought, with a collar like a tourniquet. It's a marvel any blood manages to reach his brain at all.

A minute or so after his arrival, the court completed the matter with which it was dealing and the case of the Queen against Philip Tresant was called on.

It was at this point that Mr Tidman leant sideways in Rosa's direction.

'You defending?' he hissed.

'Yes.'

'Summary trial, I gather?'

'Yes.'

76

'Good. Then we can start.'

Mr Tidman's general air and manner had set Rosa's adrenalin flowing.

Philip Tresant answered the clerk's questions audibly and without hesitation and pleaded not guilty in a firm voice. The court then granted Rosa's request that her client should be allowed to sit immediately behind her so that they could communicate without interrupting proceedings. It was no more than the usual courtesy granted where the court facilities permitted and where the defendant had answered a summons and was not in custody.

'May it please your worships,' Mr Tidman said, 'I appear for the prosecution in this case, and the defendant is represented by Miss ... er ... by Miss Epsom. ...'

'Miss Epton,' the clerk broke in. 'You're confusing her with a racecourse.'

Mr Tidman frowned, the bench maintained stony expressions and someone in the public seats at the back giggled rather loudly.

He obviously thinks a joke will put us all at ease, Rosa reflected with a sinking heart.

'As I was saying,' Mr Tidman went on briskly, 'Miss Epton defends. This is a case of simple theft. Of the theft of a five-pound note. What makes it a particularly despicable offence is that the money was stolen from the collection-plate in church.

'On Sunday, 8 September, Mr Gerald Provis and the defendant were the two sidesmen on duty at the eleven o'clock service at St Saviour's Church in this parish. Their duty involved taking round the collection-plates and handing them to the vicar, who waits to receive them at the altar. The vicar then places them on a chair at one side of the chancel. At the end of the service it is the duty of the sidesmen to take the plates into the vestry, check the money and record it and put it in a wall safe. On this particular Sunday it was the defendant who collected the two plates from the chancel chair and took them to the vestry where Mr Provis had gone directly to do the paperwork connected with the collection.

'Mr Provis had noticed a five-pound note on the defendant's plate when they processed up to the altar. When, however, the money was checked in the vestry there was no five-pound note amongst it. Later, after everybody else had left the vestry, Mr Provis taxed the defendant with the matter, but the defendant denied there had ever been a five-pound note on his plate. Mr Provis was extremely indignant and, after giving the defendant every opportunity of explaining the missing money, accused him of taking it. The defendant simply stared at Mr Provis, then turned and walked away. Conduct, your worships may feel, scarcely consistent with that of an innocent man. One would have expected him to try to resolve the matter, but he didn't. The defendant has since denied taking the money, but Mr Provis is in no doubt whatsoever that there was a five-pound note on the defendant's plate when they advanced up the aisle to the altar, and that it was missing by the time the plate was brought to the vestry. The only person who had an opportunity of taking it, apart from the defendant, was the vicar. All he does is to receive the two plates, one on top of the other, and hold them up as an offering to God before placing them on the chair at the side of the altar. The vicar has, of course, been asked about this whole distressing affair, but could offer no help. It appears that the defendant's plate was beneath the other when they were handed to him, so that he wouldn't have seen the five-pound note anyway.'

Mr Tidman took a deep breath and went on: 'Efforts to trace members of the congregation from whom the defendant collected offertory have not, I'm afraid, been productive. In the first place, there was an exceptional number of visitors from other parishes that Sunday and, second, of those regular churchgoers at St Saviour's who have been interviewed a majority declined to say anything or become involved. Your worships may feel that their lack of co-operation was a deplorable error of judgement on the part of those concerned.

'The result is that your worships have the task of trying a case in which one man's word is pitted in direct conflict against another's. I'm assuming the defendant will in due course give evidence—'

'He certainly will,' Rosa broke in quickly.

'Then, let me tell your worships why the prosecution has no doubts about the truth of its cause. Mr Provis has long been a pillar of his church and a person of proven integrity—'

'That's an extremely tendentious statement,' Rosa said, jumping to her feet. 'I'm not suggesting that Mr Provis is not a person of integrity, but to describe him at this stage as being of proven integrity is an extravagant claim to which I object.'

Mr Tidman flushed angrily. 'Miss Epston is too sensitive,' he observed with a sneer. 'However, may I now be permitted to continue? As I was saying, Mr Provis is a person of unblemished character who has no reason to make this allegation were it not true. Indeed, he has already suffered as a result of his determination to see justice done. He has been reviled by certain misguided people for doing his moral duty and bringing this matter to public notice. It required courage to do what he has done and not be deterred by the unpleasant repercussions his action was bound to arouse. If you accept his word, then the inescapable conclusion is that the defendant stole a five-pound note from the offertory plate that Sunday in September.' Mr Tidman paused and glanced about him with the air of a conjuror about to pluck a white dove from an empty top hat. 'Could he not have been mistaken? you may be asking yourselves. May he not have imagined seeing a five-pound note that never existed? The answer is a firm No to both those questions. As he and the defendant stood at the back of the church before advancing up the aisle to the altar, Mr Provis noticed a folded five-pound note on top of all the coins in the defendant's plate. It looked as if it might become dislodged, and the defendant first of all pressed it firmly down, then put a number of coins on top of it to prevent it fluttering away. That, your worships, is not something one imagines or invents.

'As I said at the outset, this was a mean and despicable theft, but you mustn't allow emotion to dictate your verdict. If the prosecution proves its case, it will be your duty to find the defendant guilty.

'I now call Mr Provis into the witness-box.'

Rosa turned to speak to Philip Tresant, who was staring with a fixed expression at the wall behind the magistrates, rather like a passenger on the deck of a storm-tossed ship uncertain how much longer he could last out.

'Are you feeling all right?' she enquired anxiously. He

nodded. 'Any comment on what's just been said to the court?' she went on.

'Gerald Provis is a self-righteous prig.'

Rosa thought this could well be so, though it didn't necessarily mean he was a liar. She was encouraged, however, that her client seemed, at least, to have come to life, despite his appearance.

Meanwhile Mr Provis had reached the witness-box and taken the oath as though making a personal declaration to the Almighty.

Under Mr Tidman's guidance he gave his evidence in a clear confident tone. It emerged exactly as the prosecuting solicitor had outlined it in his opening address, and it was with a complacent air that Mr Tidman finally resumed his seat and Rosa got up to cross-examine the witness.

She had decided that it could be counter-productive to try to prove him a liar (it would also go against her conscience in view of what she knew about her client's light-fingered propensity) and that her best hope was to show he was mistaken. Her first question to him was to set the tone.

'You don't seem to have any doubt about what you believe you saw, am I right?'

A small wintry smile flitted across the witness's face, and his eyes glinted behind his spectacles.

'It's not a question of what I believe I saw. It's what I did see.'

'Are you short-sighted?'

'Yes, that's why I wear spectacles.'

'Without them is everything blurred at close range?'

'I assure you I was wearing them that Sunday in church.'

'You haven't answered my question.'

'I've told you I'm short-sighted, but my vision is perfect with my spectacles.'

'Are you, in fact, extremely short-sighted?'

'Perhaps, but I've already explained—'

'I know. With your spectacles you can see perfectly.' Rosa broke in.

'Exactly.'

'I notice your lenses are relatively thin in the centre, but abnormally thick round the edges.'

80

The witness removed his spectacles and held them up, like an angler showing off his catch.

'There's no mystery about them,' he said with a small mirthless laugh.

What was readily apparent, however, was that without his spectacles he gave an appearance of total myopia.

'At what point did you first notice the five-pound note in the defendant's collection-plate?'

'When we were standing together at the back of the church waiting to go up to the altar.'

'Were you surprised to see it?'

'Gratified rather than surprised. We don't get many offerings of that size.'

'Did you keep your eye on it all the time you were going up the aisle together?'

'Of course not,' the witness snapped.

'When did you notice it again?'

'I'm not actually sure that I did. As we moved off towards the altar, I was aware of the defendant rearranging some coins on top of the note, but my attention was focused ahead of me.'

'I believe your church has a Christian Stewardship scheme in operation?'

'That's correct.'

'Members of the congregation seal their committed offering in a small envelope each week and place it in the offertory-plate?'

'Yes.'

'And the envelopes vary in colour from period to period?'

'Yes,' the witness said with a frown.

'Will you tell the court what colour envelopes were in use during the week of Sunday, 8 September?'

'No, I can't. Moreover, I can't see that it matters.'

'You must try to be patient with me, Mr Provis.' As she spoke, Rosa plucked a small blue envelope from beneath her papers. 'Will you accept from me that it was blue that week?' she asked sweetly.

'I suppose so.'

'So it follows that there were a number of envelopes of this colour in both collection-plates?'

'Yes, it's always a mixed collection of envelopes and cash.'

'Do you agree that the blue of this envelope is very similar to the blue of a five-pound note?' Rosa asked, holding up the envelope in one hand and a five-pound note in the other.

'Not to me, they're not,' the witness said quickly, even a shade too quickly.

'Perhaps you're a bit colour-blind as well as short-sighted?' she said, cocking her head on one side like a small bird.

'Certainly not.'

'Why are you so sure? A great many people are mildly colour-blind.'

'Well, I'm not. I wouldn't drive a car if I thought I was.'

'Nevertheless, this envelope is not, in your view, the same blue as a five-pound note?'

'You're trying to trick me,' he said after an uncomfortable pause.

'I assure you, I'm not. Just tell the court whether you think you could have mistaken one of these envelopes for a folded five-pound note?'

'Definitely not.'

'You're still as certain as you ever were?'

'Yes.'

'Do you ever make mistakes?'

'Everyone does.'

'Do you find it easy to admit yours?'

The witness gave Rosa a look of distaste.

'I hope I have the Christian humility to do so,' he said with a sniff.

'Self-righteous prig' describes him very well, Rosa reflected.

'Can you find it in your Christian humility to admit there's just a chance you're mistaken on this issue?'

He turned towards the three magistrates with the expression of somebody who has just received a sharp blow in a painful place.

'I've sworn to tell the truth,' he said in a declamatory tone, 'and I have told the truth.' He swung round to fix Rosa with a baleful stare. 'I hope that answers your question, madam.'

Rosa blinked, then quickly sat down. It was the right note on which to close her cross-examination. She was still sure her line with the witness had been the correct one. To try to brand him a liar would almost certainly have back-fired.

While she had been on her feet, she had been aware of a constant surge of restlessness to her right where Mr Tidman was sitting. She had given him no cause to interrupt, though that didn't mean he mightn't have done so. Perhaps he, too, knew what could back-fire.

He now stood up. 'I have no questions to ask in re-examination,' he said in a calculatedly offhand tone as though his witness had come through with flying colours.

As Rosa well knew, bluff and bluster were very much part of the forensic scene.

The clerk turned to whisper to the chairman, who in turn glanced at his two colleagues. It seemed that none of them wished to ask the witness any questions. Rosa thought they could be afraid of upsetting a particularly fragile applecart.

Next into the witness-box was a bored and somewhat elderly police constable who had served the summons on Philip Tresant and recorded that he didn't wish to say anything. He was followed by an obviously over-worked detective constable who had disgruntlement written all over him. Rosa suspected that both his professional and his home life were failures. She had seen the signs many times before. He gave evidence of interviewing the defendant, who had merely said he was in touch with his solicitor and had been advised not to say anything. The officer made it apparent that he wasn't bothered either way.

Mr Tidman declared that that was the case for the prosecution and shot a hungry glance at Rosa's client.

'I call Mr Tresant,' Rosa said, giving him a look of encouragement as he got to his feet.

He took the oath in a mechanical voice and then clasped the sides of the witness-box, as if for physical support.

Rosa cast him an anxious glance. She had been wondering how short she could cut his ordeal. The trouble was that she exercised no control over Mr Tidman's cross-examination and felt certain he was determined to have his money's worth. She remembered having read about a famous Queen's Counsel, later to become a well-known judge, who when defending a man on a charge of murder asked his client a single question. 'Did you murder X?' he asked. 'No' came the

83

reply, at which defending counsel sat down, leaving his client to face a somewhat more prolonged cross-examination. It was a daring ploy which took everyone by surprise, but which failed to save the client from conviction. Nevertheless, it was an opening question which might well be followed.

'Did you steal a five-pound note from the offertory-plate on Sunday, 8 September?' she now asked.

'I did not,' Philip Tresant answered firmly, seemingly galvanised by the directness of the question.

'Was there a five-pound note in the plate?'

'No. There were only coins and a number of blue envelopes.'

'What happened as you and Mr Provis started to process up the aisle with the plates?'

'One of the blue envelopes in my plate threatened to blow off, and I put two one-pound coins on top of it.'

'Why did this particular envelope behave in that manner?'

'I imagine because it contained paper money and not coins.'

'Do you remember anything else about it?'

'It had been folded lengthwise and was slowly unfolding in the plate.' He paused. 'I can see that it could, at a quick glance, have been mistaken for a five-pound note.'

Rosa nodded encouragingly. He was surpassing her expectations as a witness, even if he was visibly nervous and continued to clutch the side of the witness-box.

'What was your reaction when Mr Provis accused you of theft in the vestry?'

'I was totally stunned.'

'You heard him tell the court that you didn't say anything, but simply walked away.'

'That's true. I was too shocked to speak. And the vestry seemed the last place for any sort of unseemly argument.'

'It wasn't meant as an admission of theft on your part?'

'I hadn't stolen anything.'

'Thank you,' Rosa said and sat down.

Mr Tidman rose, straightened his tie and gave the witness a hostile glare.

'You're a thief, aren't you?' he barked.

If he had hoped to throw Philip Tresant off balance, he was disappointed.

'No, I'm not,' the witness said with a resigned sigh.

'If you're not a thief, then you're saying Mr Provis is a liar, is that right?'

'I've never said that, merely that he's mistaken.'

Rosa, who had been sitting tensely forward, relaxed. She had drummed into her client the importance of avoiding personal recriminations and had hoped he had taken in what she said. To her relief, it seemed that he had. If the prosecution resorted to confrontation tactics, that was their business and she hoped they would prove counter-productive.

'How can you mistake a five-pound note for a small blue envelope?' Mr Tidman demanded to know.

The witness gave a weary shrug. 'It was an overcast day, and the lighting is not very good in the nave of the church. I think it was quite a natural mistake in those circumstances.'

'When Mr Provis taxed you in the vestry, why didn't you offer to turn out your pockets, even let him search you?'

'I was so shocked by his accusation and aggressive manner that my only thought was to get away from him.'

'Wouldn't it have been perfectly simple to have said, "What are you talking about? There never was a five-pound note in my plate. I'll empty my pockets if that'll satisfy you"? Wouldn't that have been the natural thing to say – if it were the truth?'

'With hindsight, it might have been better, but it just didn't occur to me at the time.'

'Because you knew it would reveal you as a thief?'

'No, definitely not that.'

'Is it correct to say that you and Mr Provis have never got on?'

'I know he doesn't like me.'

'Why doesn't he like you?'

'You'd have to ask him that.'

Mr Tidman glowered at his papers to conceal his obvious sense of frustration. He belonged to the frontal-assault school of cross-examiners and became annoyed when he didn't obtain immediate results.

'Can you think of any reason why Mr Provis should have invented all this?'

Rosa was quickly on her feet.

'Surely it's not for the witness to speculate about reasons for other people's conduct. In any event, it's never been suggested that Mr Provis invented anything.'

'If Miss Epsom wants to give evidence, she'd best do it from the witness-box,' Mr Tidman snapped back.

The magistrates looked nonplussed, as they were apt to during sudden forensic skirmishes which died as quickly as they flared up. The clerk gazed indulgently at both advocates.

'And now shall we get on?' he said.

'Are you really telling the court that Mr Provis is under a totally false impression?' Mr Tidman asked in a hectoring voice.

Both the question and the tone in which it was asked told Rosa that the prosecuting solicitor had shot his bolt and must shortly sit down.

'All I'm saying is that I never stole five pounds from my offertory-plate.'

'I put it to you once again that you're a thief. That's right, isn't it?'

'No, it's not right.'

Mr Tidman sat down with an assumed air of confidence.

Rosa said she had no questions to ask in re-examination, and Philip Tresant left the witness-box. As she watched him return to his seat behind her, she marvelled that someone who looked so ill could have given such a competent performance. She could see beads of perspiration on his forehead and upper lip, which indicated the measure of his recent ordeal. She couldn't help wondering if his sickness was entirely due to mental strain. His doctor had said so, but to Rosa he had the appearance of someone mortally ill.

'You wish to address their worships, Miss Epton?' the clerk said, peering at Rosa over the top of his spectacles.

'If a theft took place,' Rosa began, 'it was indeed a despicable theft. It's difficult to think of an offence likely to arouse greater revulsion than petty theft from an offertory-plate by a respected parishioner in a position of trust.

'But, of course, it is my submission that no theft ever took place; that there was never any five-pound note in the plate.

Fortunately for your worships, it's not a case in which you have to decide who has told lies and committed brazen perjury. The defence has never suggested that Mr Provis manufactured his accusation out of malice and spite, simply that he was mistaken in what he saw. We can all make honest mistakes, the trouble being that we often become subsequently convinced that we were right.

'It's the duty of the prosecution to prove the charge beyond reasonable doubt and, if they've failed, as I submit they have, my client is entitled to be acquitted....'

Rosa went on to remind the court of Mr Provis's short-sightedness and to suggest that he was also mildly colour-blind. She invited the magistrates to compare a five-pound note with the blue envelope that had been provided as an exhibit and to see for themselves how the respective colours matched, especially when seen in a poor light and given only a casual glance.

She reminded the court of the tremendous strain her client had undergone while the charge had been hanging over him.

'I know you have listened to the evidence and to everything that's been said to you with great attention. I now urge you to find that the prosecution has not discharged its burden of proof and that the defendant must be acquitted.'

As she sat down, the magistrates gathered up their notes and retired to their room to consider their verdict. The clerk disappeared through a different door.

Mr Tidman immediately produced a small tape-recorder and began dictating. He was apparently one of those people who always had to be seen doing several things at once. A public appearance of furious activity was part of his image.

Jean Tresant left her seat at the back of the court and came and sat down next to her husband.

'How long do you think they'll be, Miss Epton?' she asked anxiously.

'I'm afraid I've no idea, but I hope not very long.'

'And what do you think their verdict will be?'

'We'll know soon enough,' Rosa said with a deprecating smile.

'But were you satisfied with the way the case went?'

87

'Yes. I think it went as well as we could have hoped.'

'Surely everyone could see that Gerald Provis was mistaken.'

'Let's hope so.'

While Jean Tresant had been speaking, she had been holding her husband's hand. He, for his part, had sat back with eyes closed and an expression of utter exhaustion.

'I wish they'd hurry up,' Jean Tresant murmured nervously.

'Why don't you go outside for a breath of air?' Rosa said.

Before she could act on Rosa's suggestion, however, there was an eruption of activity. The clerk hurried into court, followed almost immediately by the three magistrates. The chairman put on his spectacles, and the clerk quickly told Philip Tresant to stand up.

With a small preliminary cough, the chairman announced: 'After careful consideration, we feel that the prosecution has not proved its case beyond reasonable doubt and the defendant is therefore acquitted.'

Jean Tresant let out a small strangulated cry of relief, and Mr Tidman shot from the court as if he'd been told his house was on fire. The clerk smiled at Rosa.

'Hope we'll see you in our court again, Miss Epton,' he said. Then, lowering his voice, he added: 'I'm afraid Mr Tidman doesn't like losing cases.'

Rosa bowed to the magistrates, who were about to start another case, and pushed her way out of court. She noticed the rector of St Saviour's at the back and thought he looked as relieved as anyone. He clearly hadn't relished the possibility of being drawn further into a Tweedledum–Tweedledee contest.

'You were wonderful, Miss Epton,' Jean Tresant said as Rosa emerged into the foyer of the court. 'We can't thank you enough, can we, Philip?'

She was clutching her husband's arm, and he managed to give Rosa a frail smile.

'Thank you,' he said, offering her a limp handshake.

Addressing Rosa behind her husband's back, Jean Tresant went on: 'I'll take him straight home. I'm sure that now it's all over his health will start to improve within a day or so. I'll let you know.'

Rosa watched them walk away arm in arm. Her professional pride was satisfied with the result, even if other aspects niggled her. If poetic justice ever caught up with Philip Tresant, she didn't particularly wish to know.

It was a wish that was not to be fulfilled.

CHAPTER 9

MRS HENDERSON was on the warpath. Or would like to have been if there had been any weapons to hand.

More than two weeks had gone by since her friend and neighbour, Mr Gray, had disappeared and there was still no news of him. She was convinced that he was in danger, if not dead, and that the Berry woman was responsible for whatever had happened to him.

Every time she opened her front-door and looked across at Mr Gray's, her sense of outrage grew. The police had to be either incompetent or negligent not to have got anywhere with their enquiries. She had given up phoning them after Sergeant York had tersely informed her that the fact that she had reported the matter didn't entitle her to regular bulletins on the progress of the police investigation. As far as she was aware, they hadn't even yet identified the body found in Mr Gray's bed, and that was a further disgrace. All in all, her faith in the police had been severely shaken.

She was also irked by Rosa Epton's failure to keep in touch with her. Whenever she called her office, Rosa was either out or engaged with a client. Either way she didn't call back.

Each morning when the postman came she hoped to find something in her mail which would help to clear the matter up. Instead there were only bills and circulars, and letters from distant friends who were kept in touch with her busy life.

And, speaking of letters, that was a source of further irritation. Their regular postman was away, and for the past week his substitute had been apt to put letters through the wrong box. She had received two addressed to Mrs Fox, and one of hers had gone into Mr Welling's letter-box. The new postman was an Indian and, in Mrs Henderson's view, quite unsuited to the job. She would be the first to organise a church raffle in aid of the underprivileged inhabitants of the subcontinent from which he came, but to employ this particular man as a postman in what she regarded as a white stronghold was simply not good enough.

Even while these and other thoughts were passing through her mind, she heard the rattle of the letter-flap and the plop of mail on to the floor. She dried her hands on the kitchen towel and went to see what the morning delivery had brought.

There were three letters, and she stooped to pick them up. One was the telephone bill and another was a reminder that her half-yearly visit to the dentist was due. The third was addressed to Mr Arthur Welling. She quickly opened the front door in the hope of catching the postman and remonstrating with him, but he had already disappeared.

Returning to the kitchen to finish washing up her breakfast things, she gave closer scrutiny to the letter for Mr Welling. With a sense of shock she suddenly realised that she recognised the handwriting on the envelope. It was Janet Berry's. She noted the Birmingham postmark and that the letter had been posted the previous day.

She turned the envelope over, felt it, even smelt it, without becoming any wiser. It was a common self-seal white envelope and from its feel didn't contain more than a simple folded sheet of paper. She held it hopefully up to the light, but found it non-transparent.

Normally a person of brisk decision, she now found herself wondering what to do. If the police had been more forthcoming, she would have immediately notified them. Even taken the letter and handed it personally to Sergeant York. Another option was simply to put the letter through Mr Welling's door and say nothing to anybody. In between these courses of action lay a third. She could ring Mr Welling's bell and deliver it to him personally, closely observing his reaction. She might even indicate that she was aware who the writer was.

The more she thought about it, the more this seemed the most attractive course.

Her mind made up, she marched across the landing to Mr Welling's door and rang the bell. Mrs Fox was already doing her vocal scales, and Mrs Henderson shuddered. A full minute passed before the door opened to reveal an unshaven Mr Welling in a yellow towel bathrobe.

'Oh, it's you, Mrs Henderson,' he said without any show of enthusiasm. 'I thought it might be the postman.'

'In a way, it is,' she said, giving him a toothy smile. 'The silly man delivered me this letter which is addressed to you.'

She held it out, and he took it without glancing at the envelope.

'Thank you. If you'll excuse me. ...' He went to close the door.

Mrs Henderson, however, stood her ground. 'I couldn't help noticing the writing on the envelope. It's Mrs Berry's, isn't it? I wondered if there might be news of Mr Gray.' Under Arthur Welling's freezing stare, her tone faltered in its boldness.

'I'm afraid you're mistaken,' he said, giving the envelope the merest glance. 'This is a letter from my niece. Now, I really must ask you to excuse me.'

He closed the door firmly in her face, leaving her no choice but to retire to her own flat. There she made herself a fresh pot of tea and sat down to think.

She was now more certain than ever that the letter was from Janet Berry. Mr Welling's strange behaviour had confirmed this. But why had he been so quick to deny contact with her? It could only mean that they were somehow in collusion. Perhaps she actually was his niece, which would make the plot even thicker.

She decided to call Rosa and put her in possession of this new and important piece of information.

It was the day after the Tresant case, and Rosa was in her office. She listened to what Mrs Henderson had to say, then thanked her for calling.

'But what are you going to do about it?' Mrs Henderson demanded to know.

'Me? I don't propose to do anything. I suggest you inform Sergeant York. He's the person to tell.'

It didn't surprise Rosa to learn that Janet Berry was in active touch with Arthur Welling. She must let Peter Chen know before he visited the Golden Sands Club.

92

CHAPTER 10

STARSKY AND HUTCH, alias Ben Brady and Tony Lockyer, were stalking a vicious killer through the sand dunes. It was a grey misty day, and the sea had an oily sluggish appearance, as if making waves was too much of an effort. The sand was damp and clinging, and Starsky and Hutch became caked in it as they flitted from dune to dune after their will-o'-the-wisp quarry. There'd be hell to pay when they got home, but meanwhile they were joyously absorbed in their game.

They had left their cycles in the usual place and were enacting one of several episodes in their repertoire. It was a perfect time of year; the beach was as deserted as the golf-course that ran on the other side of the dunes. It was just the two of them against a shadowy villain.

Ben was eleven and Tony had just turned twelve. They had been firm friends for several years and played endlessly together. Nobody else was ever admitted to their fantasy world.

Darting forward, they hurled themselves down behind the cover of a tufted hummock. Ben glanced towards the open beach on his left.

'Look,' he exclaimed excitedly. 'What's that over against the breakwater?'

Tony peered where his friend was pointing.

'Something washed up from an old wreck,' he said with interest.

'It could be treasure.'

'Doesn't look like treasure. More like a bundle of old clothes.'

'Let's go and see,' Ben said, the vicious killer temporarily forgotten.

Together they trotted towards the breakwater about thirty yards away. The beach was strewn with bits of flotsam abandoned by the high tide.

As they neared their objective, Tony suddenly hung back.

'It's a body,' he said in a hoarse whisper. 'I can see a hand sticking out.'

Ben, the more adventurous and romantic of the two, paused, then tiptoed forward in case it was a slumbering sea-monster best left undisturbed. Tony followed at a safe distance.

'It is a body,' Ben announced shakily. Picking up a stick, he cautiously prodded it. Suddenly he jumped back a pace. 'It's an old man.'

'We'd better go and tell somebody,' Tony said. 'Wonder who he is.'

'And how he got here.'

'The tide washed him up.'

'I know that. I mean, how did he get into the sea?'

'Probably fell off a boat. Come on, let's run back to our bikes.'

As good fortune would have it, they met a policeman who happened to be on his way to investigate an attempted break-in of a boathouse.

PC Blackstock, who had two sons of about the same age, listened to them in silence before saying anything.

'You're not having me on?' he said suspiciously.

'No, honest, there really is a body,' Ben said, while Tony nodded vigorously.

'If it's some sort of hoax, you'll be sorry,' he said darkly. 'It's a serious matter making false reports to the police.'

'We know that,' Ben said with a touch of impatience. 'I promise you this is a real live body.'

'*Live* body?'

'No, a real live dead body. An old man.' Ben sounded ready to burst with exasperation.

'Come on, then. Let's hope it's still there – for your sakes.'

It was. Exactly as they had left it.

Thereafter events moved rapidly, and by early evening Rosa found herself once more in a mortuary, staring at the obscene corpse of Mr Gray.

'We'll have to wait for the pathologist to tell us how he died,' Sergeant York remarked.

'And how long he'd been in the water. Quite a time, I'd say.'

Sergeant York nodded. 'He's not a pleasant sight, is he? Even with his clothes still on. It rules out the possibility that he'd gone swimming.'

The thought of Mr Gray having gone into the water voluntarily, at his age and in the English Channel in October, was crazy, but a quick glance at the officer persuaded Rosa that his observation was seriously made.

Perhaps to a policeman nothing was too far-fetched when it came to dead bodies.

Sergeant York had promised to call Rosa the next morning and tell her the result of the post-mortem examination. He was as good as his word and was on the line within five minutes of her reaching the office.

''Morning, Miss Epton. Looks as if we have a murder enquiry on our hands,' he said with his usual directness. 'The pathologist says that Mr Gray died of asphyxia, almost certainly suffocation, and that he was dead before his body entered the water.'

'Does he give an estimate of the time he was in the water?'

'I was just coming to that. Probably about two weeks. I've consulted a nautical expert, and he tells me that there's a westerly drift along this part of the coast of approximately point six knots every twelve hours. That means the body probably entered the water somewhere in the Mongton area about two weeks ago. From there to where it was found is just over twenty miles.' He paused. 'There were marks on the body sustained after death, which points to it having fallen on to rocks, so my guess would be that it was shoved over a cliff-edge a few miles east of the town.'

'Can the pathologist say how long he'd been dead before being put into the sea?'

'Further tests are required before he can tell us that. But there was something else of interest. There were clear signs that he had been shackled while still alive. The pathologist found graze marks on his ankles and wrists which he attributes to fetters. Possibly rough rope. They're quite

95

different marks from the gashes on the body which occurred after death; presumably when he was thrown over the cliff-top.'

'It sounds as if he was held captive not far from home before being killed,' Rosa remarked.

'Yes. At the moment the pathologist can only say that he died from suffocation, and suffocation doesn't necessarily spell murder. If he was tied up, it's conceivable he could have rolled on to his face and died that way.'

'Sounds unlikely.'

'I agree. That's why we're now treating it as a murder enquiry.'

'Which means intensifying your search for Janet Berry.'

'Yes. Incidentally, Detective Chief Inspector Pickering is now in charge of the case. It's become a full-blown CID matter.'

'Does that mean you're bowing out?'

'I expect I'll still be on hand in some capacity.'

'I very much hope so.'

'Thank you, Miss Epton,' he said, clearly gratified by her comment. She was about to ring off when he went on: 'By the way, who's the chief beneficiary under Mr Gray's will? Or shouldn't I ask?'

'Dr Nagy. But keep the information to yourself for the time being, as he doesn't know yet.'

'Lucky guy. Why don't more wealthy people leave their estates to police officers? To one police officer in particular!'

'I believe rich widows have been known to.'

'Not in this part of the world.'

In the light of these events, Rosa decided to phone Peter Chen and suggest that she should accompany him when he drove down to Mongton later that day.

CHAPTER 11

Rosa never minded being driven by Peter Chen. He was a fast, but safe, driver, and his BMW gobbled the miles effortlessly where her own smaller car made heavier weather of a longer journey.

'What exactly are you going to do when we get there?' he asked as they streaked past a line of heavy vehicles on the motorway.

'I shall go to Mr Gray's flat,' she said. 'Don't worry, I shan't come near the Golden Sands Club. I have no intention of Arthur Welling seeing us together.'

'How'll you avoid the nosy neighbour?'

'Mrs Henderson? I doubt whether I'll be able to. Anyway, I probably owe it to her to tell her what's happened. I had thought I might call on Dr Nagy, but I've sent him a letter instead telling him of Mr Gray's death. He knows, of course, that he's an executor of the will, but not that he inherits practically everything.'

'But you told him that in your letter?'

'Yes, and that I was applying for a grant of probate. He'll be able to absorb the news at breakfast tomorrow.'

'How can we keep in touch while we're down there?' Peter asked after a pause.

'You can call me at Mr Gray's flat and, if for any reason I've left, I'll phone you at the club. I'll call myself Miss Woodvine.'

'Why on earth that?'

'It was my mother's name before she married.'

'My mother's name was even prettier. It was Song.'

Rosa suddenly turned and gave him a worried look. 'I've just thought of something, Peter. How'll you get in? You're not a member of the Golden Sands Club and you won't be admitted.' Her voice carried a note of mild panic.

'Who says I'm not a member?' he said complacently.

Rosa let out a sigh. 'You mean, you are?' She grinned. 'So you won't have to rely on your oriental wits after all.'

'They'd have served me just as well. But in fact, as soon as we agreed I should do a bit of nosing around, I applied for membership. I clearly know more about gaming joints than you do. You have to apply for membership and wait forty-eight hours.'

'I know. That's what I suddenly remembered.'

'I didn't even have to remember.'

Rosa decided that he deserved to have the last word on this occasion.

It was seven o'clock as they entered the outskirts of Mongton.

'I'll show you where the club is,' she said, 'then you can drive me to Southview Court.'

'Anything you say.'

'Are you going to have a serious gamble.'

'Of course. What's more, I shall win.'

Rosa was aware that when he gambled he did so in a big way. He scorned small bets as a waste of time and seldom staked less than fifty pounds on each spin of the roulette wheel.

'What time do you suggest we start back?' Rosa asked.

'Midnight?'

'I'm never going to be able to kill that amount of time,' Rosa exclaimed in dismay.

'Then, phone me when you want to leave, Miss Woodvine.'

'You'll probably be on a winning streak and refuse to budge.'

He gave an infectious laugh. 'This is a working trip. Pleasure takes second place. Anyway, I'd better not take Mr Welling's club to the cleaner's on my first visit. It wouldn't be tactful.'

'Nor likely.'

Ten minutes later he dropped her off at Southview Court.

'Take care,' he said, as he leant across and kissed her lightly on the cheek.

Rosa had hardly inserted the key in the lock of Mr Gray's

front door when Mrs Henderson's door opened.

'I thought it might be you, Miss Epton,' she said breathlessly. 'There's something in the local paper about Mr Gray's body being washed up, so I knew somebody would be here. Though quite frankly I'd expected you earlier.'

'I had a lot to do in the office before I could get away,' Rosa said, determined not to be put on the defensive.

'You'd better come in and tell me exactly what happened,' Mrs Henderson said in a tone that defied no for an answer.

'I can only tell you what you already appear to know. That Mr Gray's body was washed up about twenty miles along the coast and it's believed he'd been in the water for about two weeks.'

'The paper says he was dead before his body entered the water.'

'That's the pathologist's conclusion.'

'That wicked, wicked woman,' Mrs Henderson said in a tone of considerable indignation. 'I knew she was a bad lot from the moment I set eyes on her.'

Rosa was well acquainted with Mrs Henderson's views on Janet Berry and had no wish to hear them all over again. She detected cooking smells coming from inside her flat, which, with luck, meant Mrs Henderson was about to have her supper.

'I mustn't keep you,' she said quickly. 'You're obviously about to eat.'

'I shan't be long. Why not come in for a cup of coffee when you've finished your business at Mr Gray's?'

'I'll have to see what the time is,' Rosa replied.

'I phoned the police, as you suggested, about Mr Welling's letter from the Berry woman.'

'Good.' Rosa didn't add that Sergeant York had already told her this.

'I just hope they act on it,' Mrs Henderson remarked severely.

The smell of cooking suddenly became a smell of burning, and Mrs Henderson turned tail into her flat.

Rosa lost no time letting herself into Mr Gray's, locking the front door behind her. She went straight to the kitchen to make a cup of coffee. She'd seen a jar of Gold Blend in a cupboard on a previous visit and had also noticed a carton of long-life milk in the refrigerator.

While waiting for the kettle to boil, she opened the drawer of a Formica-topped table in search of a teaspoon. It was full of pieces of paper which, on closer scrutiny, appeared for the most part to be guarantees of the flat's various items of electrical equipment. Amongst them she noticed something in Janet Berry's handwriting. It was headed 'Mrs K.'s recipe for strawberry shortcake'. There followed a lengthy pencilled scrawl on how to make this delicacy. From the involved instructions it had to be delicious.

Turning the piece of paper over, Rosa suddenly frowned. It was a bill from Melissa's Foodstore of 49 Main Avenue, Beachdean, made out to 'Berry, 14 Clifftop Rise', and was for such staple items as bread, sugar, butter, eggs and cereal, amounting in all to £4.78.

With a feeling of distinct excitement, Rosa fetched the telephone directory from Mr Gray's study and confirmed the existence of Melissa's Foodstore with the address and telephone number shown on the bill. She then glanced down the columns of Berrys in the directory, but failed to find anyone of that name who claimed 14 Clifftop Rise as their address.

She took her cup into the living room to sit down and think. She didn't have to think for very long, however, before she became convinced that it was the address where Mr Gray had been held hostage before meeting his death. She had driven through Beachdean and knew it as a haphazard growth of weekend and holiday homes, with a small nucleus of permanent residents who lived there all the year round, braving the winter gales and the angry seas that pounded the foot of the cliff. It lay on the coast road a few miles east of Mongton.

She noted that the bill was dated a few weeks before Mr Gray had disappeared, which seemed to indicate that the supplies had not been ordered with him in mind. Who, then? It seemed unlikely that Janet Berry went there when she had time off just to have a picnic. That meant somebody was living there all the time. There was only one way to resolve the mystery and that was to go and investigate.

She turned once more to the telephone directory, before

calling the Golden Sands Club.

'I'd like to speak to Mr Chen, please,' she said. 'I believe he's in the club. He's a member.'

'Chen, did you say? Would he be the Chinese gentleman who came in a short while ago?'

'Yes, could you page him, please?'

'Who's speaking?'

'Miss Woodvine.'

Rosa heard muffled voices as a hand was placed over the mouthpiece; then more clearly: 'Will Mr Chen come to reception, please?'

A couple of minutes later Peter came on the line.

'Hi,' he said, in a way that indicated that any conversation could be overheard.

'I'm sorry to interrupt you, Peter, but something's happened.'

'No bother. I was having a drink. I hadn't reached the tables. What can I do for you?'

'Can you pick me up at the flat as soon as possible? I'll explain everything then. I'll wait downstairs by the entrance so that you needn't get out of the car.'

'See you shortly, then.'

Rosa finished her coffee, washed the cup and departed with as much stealth as possible. Fortunately, Mrs Fox was singing fortissimo, which drowned lesser sounds; and, to Rosa's relief, Mrs Henderson's door remained firmly closed.

She didn't have long to wait before Peter Chen drew up and she got quickly into his car.

'So what's all the excitement?' he asked as he pulled away from the kerb.

Rosa told him.

'Which way do I go for Beachdean?' he enquired when Rosa finished.

There was little traffic about, and it took them less than fifteen minutes to get there.

'What a dump!' he remarked when Rosa told him to stop.

'I wonder where Main Avenue is?' she said.

'It was that last turning on the left. I saw the nameplate on the ground propped against the Chinese takeaway. Anyway, I thought we wanted Clifftop Rise.'

101

'I thought we'd begin by locating Melissa's Foodstore.'

Throwing her an amused smile, he rapidly reversed the car and turned into Main Avenue.

'It's probably in that parade of shops on the right,' he said a moment later.

They found it sandwiched between a newsagent and an ice-cream parlour. All three were closed, which was hardly surprising on a dark October night.

'I'll go into the Chinese takeaway and enquire where Clifftop Rise is,' Peter said as he once more turned the car.

'Can we try to find it without asking?' Rosa said. 'It may be better if we're not seen in the area. Could you park somewhere and then we can explore on foot? From the address, it must be close to the cliff-edge, which means on the other side of the main road.'

'I'd have put on my thermal underwear if I'd known,' Peter observed with a sigh.

'Why don't we take one of those turnings that lead towards the cliff and feel our way?'

'As long as we don't feel our way right over the edge,' he said as he parked behind a dumper truck close to a building site.

They were about twenty yards from the main road and darted quickly across it.

'Look,' Peter said, pointing to a turning just ahead. '"Green Lane, leading to Clifftop Rise." We've struck lucky.'

The first fifty yards of Green Lane were tarmac, but thereafter it became a rutted track of loose stones and potholes. Soon they could see the protective wire fence that ran along the top of the cliff.

'Clifftop Rise to the left,' Peter said as they reached a T junction just short of the fence.

There were three bungalows huddled closely together at the junction. Two were in total darkness, one showed a faint yellow glow round the edge of a side-window.

'So which is number fourteen?' he said with a touch of impatience.

'There's another bungalow ahead,' Rosa remarked, pointing to the looming shape of a squat building thirty yards in front of them. It stood isolated and was separated from the other three by rough ground.

102

'Give me Siberia any day,' Peter murmured as they made their way along the uneven track. 'You're right,' he cried out a moment later, pausing beside a wooden stake in the ground with a cross-piece on which the number '14' was roughly painted.

As they came up to the bungalow they could see it was constructed of wooden shingles, with a dilapidated fence running round its perimeter. A thick hedge ran at an oblique angle and acted as a windshield.

'We'd better find a way in,' Peter said eagerly.

'Let's make sure there's nobody about,' Rosa remarked, uncomfortably aware that at any moment she was going to put herself on the wrong side of the law.

'OK, you wait here and I'll have a quick look around.'

'Don't be long.'

'I'll be back before you can count up to ten,' he said, melting away from her side.

Rosa turned her back to the south-westerly wind and hugged herself to stay warm as she listened to the waves hurling themselves ceaselessly against the rocks below. She refused to believe that there could ever be more than a few weeks each year when living in Clifftop Rise was tolerable. She glanced over her shoulder at the wire fence that snaked its way along the top of the cliff. In her mind's eye she could see Mr Gray's body being manhandled over it and then toppled off the cliff-edge. The perpetrator of this dark deed, however, remained faceless.

She peered at the outline of the bungalow that was number 14. Peter had disappeared round the back, picking his way fastidiously over the rough ground. Poor Peter! He had come dressed for an evening at a casino and found himself on a breaking-and-entering expedition.

She was suddenly aware of light reflected behind her and looked round to see a car turning out of Green Lane into Clifftop Rise. She quickly stepped further back from the so-called road to avoid being seen. Her immediate assumption was that somebody was visiting one of the three bungalows at the junction. Maybe it was one of the residents returning home. The car didn't stop, but came slowly on, its headlights sweeping the landscape as it lurched along the track.

Rosa made a dash for better cover, also to alert Peter. She found a gaping hole in the perimeter fence and clambered through.

'Peter, Peter,' she called out urgently.

His voice coming immediately behind her made her jump.

'You can't have counted up to ten,' he said. 'I was just coming back to tell you that the kitchen window looks our best way in. . . .'

'There's a car coming,' Rosa said, clutching his arm.

'So there is,' he remarked with apparent unconcern. 'Come on, we'll get behind the hedge.'

They had scarcely gained cover when the car came to a halt in front of the bungalow and somebody got out. A moment later they heard footsteps on the wooden veranda at the front of the bungalow.

Taking Rosa's hand, Peter led the way to the end of the hedge and peered round.

'It's somebody with a key,' he said. 'They've gone inside. Know anyone who has a Ford Sierra?' he went on.

'Several people, but none of them likely to be visiting Clifftop Rise.'

'He hasn't turned on any lights, but he's got a torch.'

'Why do you say *he*?'

'Because it seems more likely than *she*.'

'Don't forget Janet Berry.'

'I'm not. Hang on, he's leaving again already. Quick, see if you recognise him.'

Rosa edged forward and poked her head between the hedge and Peter Chen's protective shoulder. She saw somebody hurry back to the car and get in.

'I agree it looks like a man,' she said. 'But it's too dark to recognise faces.'

The engine was started and the car's lights came on, but nothing happened.

'He's stuck,' Peter whispered gleefully. 'His rear wheels are spinning.'

As he spoke, the driver got out and walked round to the back of the car, where he appeared to be examining the ground. After a moment he moved to the front and repeated the operation.

104

For a couple of seconds he stood in the full glare of the headlights.

'It's Arthur Welling,' Rosa said excitedly.

He got back into the car, the engine roared above the sound of breaking waves and suddenly it lurched forward. Turning it with a certain recklessness, he headed back along Clifftop Rise towards the junction with Green Lane, where he turned right and disappeared.

'I think he got into a bit of a panic,' Peter remarked. 'Probably thought he wouldn't get his car free without help, and I imagine that's the last thing he'd have wanted.' He put an arm round Rosa's waist. 'Now it's our turn to go in.'

'I wonder what he came for?' Rosa said in a thoughtful tone.

'With luck we'll find out. Whatever it was didn't keep him long.'

Peter led the way round the side of the bungalow to a window at the back overlooking a patch of weeds and rubble. Taking a small penknife from his pocket, he inserted it between the window and its frame. A single sharp tug and the window was open.

'I'll get in and then give you a hand.'

'If I'd known what was in store, I'd have worn slacks,' Rosa said.

'And I wouldn't have worn expensive Italian shoes.'

Expensive shoes or not, he disappeared through the window with the agility of a gazelle and then leant out to help Rosa. 'Get on to the sill,' he said, 'and I'll lift you over the sink.'

'Let's draw the curtains before we switch on any lights.'

From the kitchen they moved through a doorway into a room which faced on to the veranda. There were thick curtains which hung to the floor and which, Rosa imagined, were as necessary for keeping out draughts as for anything else. A door led into a short passage on the far side of which was a room with an unmade double bed.

The whole interior had an untidy and desolate air. The sink was full of unwashed plates and cutlery, and there was a filthy saucepan on the stove with the remnants of baked beans adhering to its interior. While Rosa gazed around, Peter explored further.

'Have a look at this,' he called to her.

He was standing in a slip of a room next to the bedroom. It had no window and was lit by a low-power naked bulb. Its only furniture was a camp-bed on which lay a heap of twisted blankets and a dirty cushion.

'Obviously the guest room,' he remarked.

Rosa suddenly knelt down and swept her hand beneath the bed.

'And I can tell you who the recent guest was,' she said, holding up some pieces of old rope. 'This is where they kept Mr Gray before killing him and throwing him over the cliff.'

'They?'

'There must have been more than one person involved. But what were they up to, Peter? Why did they need to abduct him and hold him here?'

'The answer to that lies with the body found in his bed. Identify that and you have the answers to lots of other questions.'

Rosa shook her head in bewilderment. 'But what's it all about?' she exclaimed in a tone of frustration. She glanced around the cheerless surroundings. 'And there's another thing, Peter. All that mess and those unwashed dishes. Janet Berry was a particularly clean person. She would never have lived in that sort of squalor.'

'So what do we do now?' Peter enquired with a shrug.

'I must let Sergeant York know what we've discovered.'

'You'd better decide exactly how you're going to tell him. He may be pleased to have the information, but he's unlikely to congratulate you on the way you obtained it. The police can be touchy about these things.'

'I know.'

'Anyway, let's get back to the car and have a think.'

'Do you want to return to the Golden Sands Club?'

'No need. We've found out more about Arthur Welling here than I'd have done by staying in his club. I'll come back another time and take a slice of his profits.'

Rosa felt that not only public duty, but also a sense of personal obligation, required her to let Sergeant York know as soon as possible what had happened.

106

She decided she would tell him the whole story, save that she and Peter had broken into the bungalow. To do that might stretch his indulgence beyond its limit. Moreover, it wasn't strictly necessary for him to know. After all, the police would be making their own much more thorough search of 14 Clifftop Rise.

She was glad now that she had thrown the pieces of rope back under the camp-bed, where they would be found in their original position. She hoped that she and Peter hadn't left too many fingerprints around – or, more important, hadn't obliterated any of those already there. Before they departed, Peter had closed the kitchen window from inside and they had gone out through the front door, which was fitted with a single Yale lock.

As they drove back along the coast road and into Mongton, Rosa stared in thoughtful silence at the serried ranks of white-crested waves sweeping in as if eager to reach the well-lit shore.

She recalled Sergeant York having said he would be on night duty this week and assumed he'd have clocked on by the time they reached the station. It was just after ten o'clock. She and Peter had already agreed it would be better for her to go in alone.

'I know our police are wonderful,' Peter had said on the way back, 'but there are times when my love and admiration aren't always reciprocated. I feel this could be one of them.'

At the station Rosa gave her name to the officer on reception duty and sat down to await Sergeant York's arrival. About three minutes later he appeared.

'What are you doing here at this hour, Miss Epton?' he enquired in an amiable but slightly guarded tone.

'A friend was driving down to Mongton and I decided to hitch a ride,' she said lightly. 'It seemed an opportunity to start sorting out Mr Gray's things.'

'And you came across something of interest?' he broke in.

'Yes, this,' she replied, handing him the Melissa Foodstore bill. 'The writing on the back is Janet Berry's.'

'"Mrs K.'s recipe for strawberry shortcake,"' he read in a puzzled tone. 'Is that supposed to have some relevance?'

'It connects Mrs Berry with the items supplied by the shop.

107

The thing to note is the name and address shown on the bill.'

'"Berry, 14 Clifftop Rise,"' he murmured to himself. Then, looking up and meeting Rosa's gaze, he said: 'What's your theory, Miss Epton?'

'As a matter of fact I've just been out to Beachdean,' Rosa said in what she hoped was a disarming tone. 'I thought I'd go and see if 14 Clifftop Rise existed....'

'Why shouldn't it exist?' Sergeant York asked sharply.

'No reason at all. Anyway, it does. It looked deserted, but while I was there a car arrived and somebody went inside. It was Arthur Welling.'

'Now, that *is* interesting! Did he see you?'

'No. He wasn't there more than two or three minutes and then left.'

'Were you alone, Miss Epton?'

'The friend who drove me down was with me.'

'Did your friend see Mr Welling, too?'

'He saw him, but didn't know who he was as he'd never met him.'

'And all this happened this evening?'

'Less than an hour ago.'

'I gather you think Mr Gray may have been held there before being killed.'

'It seems a reasonable inference. But you'll get a much better idea when you search the place.'

Sergeant York fixed her with a hard stare but kept his thoughts, whatever they might be, to himself.

'Anything else to tell me?' he said at last.

'No, that's all. I remember you'd said you would be on night duty this week, so I thought I'd drop by before returning to London.'

'I'm very glad you did. I'll pass the information on to Detective Chief Inspector Pickering. It could be the break we're looking for. It certainly provides us with a bit of leverage against Arthur Welling, which won't come amiss.' He picked up the Melissa Foodstore bill and reread the reverse side. 'I'm rather partial to shortcake,' he remarked. 'I think I'll get my wife to try this recipe.'

108

CHAPTER 12

It was two days later that Rosa received a letter from Mr Gray's bank manager.

Dear Miss Epton,
Thank you for your letter of 29 October informing me of the unfortunate death of Mr Gray. I note that you and Dr Nagy are the executors of his will and that you will send the bank a copy of probate once it has been obtained. I shall be pleased to open an executors' account at this branch if you so desire. Meanwhile I enclose a number of forms which are self-explanatory and shall be glad if you will complete and return these at your convenience.

I note from your letter that Mr Gray's death is the subject of police enquiries.

Finally, I should mention that the bank holds a sealed cash-box on behalf of Mr Gray. He deposited it here not long after his arrival in the area and his opening an account at this branch. As far as I am aware it has never been opened, and I have no knowledge of its contents. I shall be glad to hand it to you against receipt whenever you wish to collect it.

Yours sincerely,
A. Worsley
Manager

Rosa didn't feel very inclined to waste half a day travelling down to Mongton and back; on the other hand, news of the cash-box excited her curiosity.

She telephoned the bank to ask if she could send a

messenger to collect it, and after a certain hesitation it was agreed that this would be in order, provided the person concerned carried her signed authority.

It was then that Ben was duly instructed and sent on his way. Ben, who was twenty-one, was the firm's outdoor clerk, but in practice undertook any duties assigned to him, including tea-making. He had been a one-time client of Rosa's, who after a spell in Borstal had come knocking on Snaith & Epton's door asking for a job. After a good deal of hesitation he had been taken on, and it was fair to say that neither side seemed to have regretted the decision.

There was nothing Ben enjoyed more than what he regarded as special assignments.

'I want you to go down to Mongton, Ben, and pick up something from the Southern Counties Bank,' Rosa said, shortly after agreeing the arrangement.

'What, straightaway, Miss Epton?' he asked.

'Yes.'

'Brill.'

Rosa knew this to be short for 'brilliant' and to be Ben's current vogue word for expressing pleasure.

'Come back in ten minutes and I'll have a letter of authority for you to hand to the bank.'

'What is it I'm supposed to be picking up?'

'A cash-box. I've no idea what's in it, but you'd better guard it with your life.'

'Could be full of diamonds, you mean?'

'I doubt it, but when I say I've no idea I mean it. So don't go and leave it anywhere.'

Ben looked hurt. 'Be fair, Miss Epton. Am I likely to?'

'If I thought you were, I'd hardly be sending you, would I? Incidentally, how are things with Pauline? You've not mentioned her recently.'

Pauline was Ben's steady girl-friend of the past two years.

'She's fine,' he said with a slightly clouded expression.

'Good. She's a nice girl, Ben. You want to hang on to her.' Rosa was fond of Ben and felt a special responsibility for his welfare.

'Trouble is', Ben said, 'she hangs on to me a bit too tightly. She's getting broody, and I don't want to know.' His

110

expression cleared. 'But she's still one in a hundred.'

Trust Ben not to exaggerate, Rosa reflected wryly.

'There'll probably be a further small job when you get back,' Rosa said as he turned to go.

'Such as?'

'Opening the box.'

Ben grinned. 'No problem. No problem at all, Miss Epton.'

Four hours later he was back in Rosa's office, looking pleased with himself. Opening the haversack he was carrying, he pulled out a dark green metal box, which had strips of adhesive tape all round it. A label tied to the handle on top read: 'Property of Mr Vernon Gray.'

'The bank handed it over without any bother?' Rosa enquired.

'They were a bit stuffy at first, but after I'd produced the letter you gave me and said I didn't have all day a couple of clerks went down to the strong-room to get it. When I saw two of 'em go, I thought they must bring up a cabin trunk at least, but it seems they're only allowed into the strong-room in pairs. I suppose it's so they can watch each other and make sure nobody nicks a tiara or two.'

'I doubt if we'll find any tiaras in this box,' Rosa remarked. 'Can you remove all the sticky tape?'

Despite rather delicate-looking hands, Ben had extremely strong wrists and fingers whose dexterity any violinist would have envied. He ripped off all the tape in one continuing movement.

''Fraid it's locked, Miss Epton,' he said as he tried to lift the lid. 'Got a key?'

Rosa shook her head. 'Did the bank mention a key?'

'No. Never asked them, I'm afraid.'

'I expect the key's somewhere in Mr Gray's flat. Do you think we can open it without one?'

''Course we can. Want me to have a go?' Rosa nodded. 'I'll just get a suitable tool,' he said and dashed out of the room, returning a couple of minutes later with two screwdrivers and a pair of pliers. 'These are all I could find, but they should do the trick between them.' He gave Rosa a quizzical glance. 'You don't mind the lock being busted beyond repair?'

'I don't mind what happens as long as you open it.'

111

It took Ben several minutes of exertion and dark muttering before the lid finally flew open.

'Just a lot of old papers,' he said in disgust as they peered at the contents. 'Well, I'd better leave you to it, Miss Epton. I've got some briefs to deliver to the Temple and then I've promised to take Pauline out for a meal tonight. Her mum had a spectacular win at bingo the other evening and has given us a hundred quid. Mind you, we're not spending it all on a nosh-up.'

'Enjoy your evening, Ben, and thanks for going down to Mongton.'

With Ben's departure, Rosa started to examine the documents in the box.

The first was a death certificate relating to Adèle Constance Vinter who had died at 48 Larchfield Road, Benny Common, near Reading, on 14 November 1966. The cause of death was given as cerebral haemorrhage.

Rosa stared at the certificate, wondering who Adèle Vinter had been and why Mr Gray had a copy of her death certificate locked securely away in his bank.

The next document she took out and unfolded was a marriage certificate showing that George Vinter had married Adèle Constance Mott at All Saints' Church, Balham, on 7 July 1930. So what?

The final item was a birth certificate relating to George Vinter, who had been born in a hospital at Stoke-on-Trent on 23 April 1905.

Rosa laid the three documents out on her desk as if they were part of a jigsaw and stared at them.

Quite suddenly something exploded in her mind. April 23rd was St George's Day, but much more vitally it was Mr Gray's birthday. She recalled his having told her (one of the few pieces of personal information he had imparted) and that she had remarked it was surprising his parents hadn't named him after the patron saint. She recalled, too, the curiously enigmatic little smile he had given her when she made her observation.

Could Vernon Gray really be George Vinter? Speculation now suddenly became certainty as she remembered how often people who assumed fresh identities adopted a sort of code name. In this instance he had reversed his initials. G.V. became V.G.

She was so absorbed in thought that she didn't hear her partner, Robin, come into her room.

'You've got a full house there,' he remarked, looking over her shoulder. 'A birth, a marriage and a death certificate. Anyway, who are the Vinters?'

Rosa told him her theory, and he became thoughtful.

'It's as if you've peeled off one onion skin without yet reaching the heart. But at least you've got something to work on.'

Rosa nodded keenly. 'I'll drive down to Benny Common in the morning. I'm not due in court till the afternoon; 48 Larchfield Road will be my starting-point.'

'I hope it doesn't also prove to be a cul-de-sac,' Robin said wryly. 'But it's twenty years since Mrs Vinter died there and you'll probably find the house has changed hands several times.'

'It's still the obvious starting-point,' Rosa said determinedly. 'I'm not expecting it also to be the finishing-post.'

Rosa was on her way soon after eight o'clock the next morning. Within fifteen minutes she was heading westwards along the M4. Heathrow came and went on her left side, followed a few miles further on by a picture-postcard view of Windsor Castle.

A study of the map had shown Benny Common to be west of Reading and within three miles of the motorway turn-off junction. The weather was fine and, at that hour of the morning the bulk of the traffic was going in the opposite direction towards London. All this meant that she made good time and reached her destination in little over an hour. She stopped outside a newsagent and went in to ask the way to Larchfield Road.

'You can't miss it,' said a ginger-moustached man behind the counter, with what turned out to be unjustified optimism.

Eventually, however, after obtaining two further sets of directions, Rosa arrived at the road she was looking for. Number 48 was about a hundred yards along on the left where the road began to curve away to the right. The houses

113

belonged to the immediate post-war period and showed their age, though most of them had neat well-tended gardens in front. It was a middle-class area with the slides under it. Rosa thought it probable that those who made money quickly left for greener pastures.

She parked outside number 48 and walked up the path to the front door. She rang the bell and waited. The door was opened by a woman of about thirty, who looked grossly overweight, a condition her clothes did little to hide. She was wearing a tight sweater and a pair of slacks that would have fitted the hind legs of an elephant. A small child peered round her with large solemn eyes.

Rosa gave the woman a bright smile. 'I wonder if you can help me . . .' she began.

'If you're from one of those religious sects, the answer's no.'

'I'm not. I'm a solicitor from London and I'm trying to trace somebody who once lived at this address.' She handed the woman a card showing the firm's name and address, as well as her own.

'Oh, that's all right, then; but we get so many cranky people coming to the door trying to save our souls, I thought you must be another. Who is it you're enquiring about?'

'A Mr and Mrs Vinter. Mrs Vinter died at this address in 1966.'

'I've never heard the name. We've only been here a year. The people we bought from were called Gifford.'

'Had the Giffords lived here long?'

'About five years, I think. They moved to Wales, but I can't tell you their address.'

'Do you know of anyone in the street who's lived here for twenty years or more?'

The woman shook her head in a doubtful manner while the child gave Rosa a raking look.

'Properties are changing hands all the time. It's really just a dormitory town. I know I wouldn't want to spend the rest of my days here.' She paused. 'I should think Proctor's, the newsagent, would be your best bet for information about former residents.'

'Is that the shop with the ginger-moustached assistant?'

'That's Fred, the son. His father's the person you want to

114

talk to. He doesn't usually appear till later in the morning, but he lives in the flat above the shop. Ask to see him.'

'Thanks, I will. You've been most helpful,' Rosa said. She gave the child a friendly smile, which, however, drew no response.

She got back into the car and retraced her steps to the shop where she had originally sought directions.

'Hello again. Find Larchfield Road quite easy, did you?' Fred enquired genially.

'Let's just say I found it,' Rosa said with a faint smile. 'I wondered if I could have a word with your father? I gather he's lived here quite a time.'

'Came here after the Second World War. Started up this business as soon as he came out of the forces. There's nothing he can't tell you about Benny Common.'

'Then, I'm sure he'll be able to help me,' Rosa said, and went on to tell ginger-moustached Fred of her quest.

'If you hang on for a moment, I'll nip upstairs and see if he's dressed. If anyone comes into the shop, tell them where I've gone.'

He opened a door behind him and disappeared up a flight of stairs. A couple of minutes later he was back again.

'Yes, that's OK, if you'd like to go up. Dad hasn't had a shave yet, but I don't suppose that'll worry you. You've not come to take his picture, have you?' he added with a laugh. He opened the door and gave a shout. 'The lady's on her way up, Dad.'

Waiting at the top of the stairs was a small benign-looking man who could easily have passed himself off as one of Snow White's dwarfs.

'Come in, miss,' he said, waving an arm towards the kitchen. 'You don't mind, do you? But it's the warmest room, and my circulation's none too good these days.' When they were seated on either side of the kitchen table, he went on: 'I gather you're enquiring about people who used to live at 48 Larchfield.'

'Mr and Mrs Vinter,' Rosa said with a hopeful smile.

'Let's see now, they came between the Chattertons and the Winslows. If I remember right, they used to have the *Telegraph* and the *Express*.' He gave a chuckle. 'Mr Chatterton was a bit of a Red and used to take the *Daily Worker*. One of the paper-boys refused to deliver it, said his father told him not to, the spotty-faced little snot.'

'How long did the Vinters live there?' Rosa asked, encouraged by the flow of information.

'I'd say about eight or ten years. Mr Vinter didn't stay on more than a few months after his wife's death.'

'Do you know where he moved to?'

'I think it was somewhere nearer his work – not that I ever saw him again.'

'Where did he work?' Rosa asked keenly.

'Over Brackingham way. I think he was in the accounts department of a factory. He used to drive over every day.'

'Do you know the name of the factory?'

'No. He never told me, and you learn not to ask too many questions if you don't want to lose customers. I have an idea, however, that they made furniture. I think he must have said something once to give me that impression.'

'What sort of man was he?'

'What, Mr Vinter? He was tall and thin. A very respectable gentleman.'

'If he's the person I believe he was, he's dead. I wonder if you'd mind looking at a photograph. . . . The only thing is, it's not a very pleasant one. It was taken after he'd been in the sea for a couple of weeks. But I'd be grateful if you'd give it a quick look and tell me if it bears any resemblance to the Mr Vinter who used to live at 48 Larchfield Road.'

The old man held out his hand as Rosa took the photograph from her handbag. It was one taken at the mortuary, which Sergeant York had given her. Rosa had trimmed it, so that only the head and shoulders appeared.

'I'd better put on my specs,' he said, rummaging in a pocket.

Rosa watched him as he gazed hard and long at the photo in his hand.

'I'm afraid he's not a very pleasant sight.'

'Don't let that worry you, miss. I was in the navy through the last war and saw my share of drowned men. I just want to make sure before I speak. It's twenty years since he left the district, and people's faces change in that time.' After a

116

further scrutiny, he laid the photograph down on the table and said: 'Yes, that's Mr Vinter all right.'

'You're quite sure, Mr Proctor?'

'I never say I'm sure of anything if I'm not,' he said with a note of rebuke.

'I'm sorry, I didn't mean to sound rude. It's my lawyer's caution, I'm afraid.'

'That's all right, miss. No offence taken.'

'I'm very grateful for your help,' Rosa said, retrieving the photograph and putting it back in her bag. 'I must now try to find out where Mr Vinter worked.'

Mr Proctor scratched the back of his head and assumed a thoughtful air. 'I feel sure it was somewhere that made furniture.' He suddenly gave the top of his head a slap. 'Yes, I remember now. We were talking about chairs and I remarked that often the more comfortable they looked, the more uncomfortable they were to sit on, and he laughed and said his boss had spent years designing a dining-room chair that guests wouldn't want to get up from. And I said I wasn't too sure that would be an advantage. After all, you don't want your guests sitting round your table all night, drinking all your port and brandy.' He chuckled. 'At one time I was chief steward in the senior officers' mess in an aircraft-carrier.' He paused. 'Funny my suddenly remembering all that. About the chairs, I mean.'

'It's another helpful titbit,' Rosa said as she got up to go.

After thanking the old man again for his help, she went back downstairs and into the shop.

'Dad able to help you?' ginger Fred enquired.

'Yes, a lot. He's got a remarkable memory.'

Fred rolled his eyes in mock despair. 'Once you start him off he'll tell you the name of everyone we've ever delivered papers to. It's a matter of pride to him.' He shook his head slowly. 'It's incredible the amount of useless information people stuff their heads with.'

Rosa couldn't help wishing there were more Mr Proctors about, their heads stuffed with apparently useless information.

It wasn't yet ten-thirty, and she decided she would return to London via Brackingham. It wouldn't add much to her

117

journey and she hoped it might prove a visit as fruitful as the one to Benny Common.

As she approached the town she noticed a turning to 'Brackingham Industrial Estate' and reckoned that would be as likely a place as any to find a furniture factory. About half a mile along the road she reached it, a complex of buildings with service roads and a general landscaped effect, apart from the surrounding high wire fence. A bit further on she came to the entrance, protected by a striped barrier. A uniformed security guard stared at her from his hut. As he showed no sign of moving, Rosa got out of her car and went up to him.

'I'm looking for a furniture factory,' she said. 'Is there one here?'

'What's the name of it?'

'I don't know. All I do know is that it makes furniture.'

He gave her an unfriendly stare.

'There's no such plant here,' he said in a tone that matched his look. Pointing at a board at the far side of the entrance, he added: 'There are all the names of the firms located here.'

Rosa turned and studied the list. Most of those on it revealed their line of business in their names and certainly none indicated any interest in furniture-making. There were two, however, that gave nothing away. F. Grainger Ltd and Appleyard Industries Ltd.

'Neither of them make furniture?' she asked, pointing at their names.

'Graingers make toys and Appleyards turn out television aerials,' he said without a smile.

'I seem to have reached a dead end,' Rosa remarked forlornly. 'Sorry to have troubled you.'

'There used to be a furniture factory about a mile out of town on the London road,' he now said in a relenting tone.

'Used to be?'

'That's right. It's now a warehouse for a removal firm. Caring Removals they're called.'

'I'll try my luck there. Thanks.'

She was aware of the guard's gaze following her back to her car and as she drove away. Perhaps there was an alert on and he was waiting for somebody to try to blow up the place. At all

118

events, he was certainly more conscientious than many security guards she had come across.

A quarter of an hour later she pulled up outside Caring Removals Ltd. Beneath their name appeared the confident slogan 'We really do take care'.

By contrast with the industrial estate she'd just left, Rosa had difficulty in finding anyone about. She peeped through windows and rattled locked doors to no avail and was wondering what to do next when a youth in a pair of crisp green overalls came round a corner of the building. He was carrying a motor-cycle helmet.

'Excuse me,' Rosa called out. 'Can you tell me where the office is, please?'

'We don't have an office here. This is only our warehouse. Benny Common's where you want; that's where all the business is done. They'll be pleased to help you. Moving house, are you?'

'No. I'm only trying to find out if there used to be a furniture factory on this site.'

''Fraid I don't know. I've only worked for Caring a couple of months. I just came over to check a load we're taking down to Devon tomorrow. Me and Bob, that is,' he added with a note of pride.

'Who do you suggest I speak to at your office in Benny Common?'

'You could try Mr Dixon.'

'What's his position?'

'Transport manager.'

'Has he been with the firm a long time?'

'Not as long as Miss Dove.'

'Who's she?'

'She's the secretary. She knows everything.'

Thanking him for his help, Rosa returned a trifle disconsolately to her car. She supposed she had no right to have expected her luck to continue, but nevertheless she felt frustrated. It was as if she'd been on a paper chase and had suddenly lost the trail.

Before driving off she made a note of the Caring Removals telephone number.

It was nearly half-past five before she got back to the office

119

from court, but with luck there might still be somebody answering the telephone at Caring Removals. She dialled the number, and a female voice replied.

'May I speak to Miss Dove, please.'

'Miss Dove speaking,' the voice said in a tone that struck a comfortable balance between aloofness and a total readiness to help all comers. After Rosa had explained her quest, Miss Dove said: 'It certainly used to be a furniture factory. J. T. Furniture Ltd was the name, but that's about all I can tell you. They went bankrupt, and we acquired the premises from the receiver. We didn't have any personal contact at all with the previous owners. They'd gone before we came on the scene.' She paused. 'I take it that it's the owner you wish to trace?'

'Not necessarily. Just somebody who knew the workforce during the sixties and seventies.'

'I don't think they employed more than a couple of dozen people. It was a small family business that had the misfortune to crash. Though I'm afraid I don't know anything about the circumstances.'

'Do you know the name of the family? That might help me.'

'No, I don't, but I might be able to find out something for you, Miss Epton. If you care to give me your telephone number, I'll call you when I have any information.'

'I'd be most grateful,' Rosa said, her hopes once more on an upward swing.

She had recognised Miss Dove's voice as belonging to the sort of employee any firm was lucky to have. Loyal, reliable, sane and conscientious. Rather like Stephanie in their own office, except that Stephanie's rather nasal tones would never tell one all that.

It was with a sigh of relief that she put papers into her briefcase for court the next morning and left to go home. All in all it had been a satisfactory day, even to the extent of getting a client off a charge of obstructing the police during the course of his one-man demonstration on the pavement outside a pub that had refused to serve him on the grounds he was already too well refreshed.

CHAPTER 13

ARTHUR WELLING sat facing Detective Chief Inspector Pickering and Sergeant York across a table that was bare apart from a small tape-recorder. He had never liked police stations and he felt distinctly uncomfortable, which suited the officers.

'This time let's have the truth,' Pickering said. 'What were you doing at 14 Clifftop Rise?'

'I haven't even said I was there.'

'We know you were, so don't prevaricate.'

'Who says I was?'

'You were seen driving up, getting out of your car and letting yourself into the bungalow.'

'Whoever says it was me is mistaken.'

'Are they also mistaken about your car getting stuck and the wheels spinning so that you had to get out?'

Arthur Welling was unable to hide his surprise and looked momentarily shaken.

'It's all an invention,' he said without much attempt at conviction.

'We know you're in touch with Janet Berry,' Pickering went on remorselessly. 'We want to find her. Where is she?'

'I've no idea.'

'But you admit to being in contact with her?'

'She may have been in contact with me, but that's not the same thing.'

'May have?'

'All right, she has been. I suppose my nosy neighbour told you.'

'Why did you tell Mrs Henderson it was a letter from your niece?'

'Because it was none of her bloody business,' he said viciously.

'The letter was postmarked Birmingham. What was the actual address?'

'There wasn't one on it.'

'What was she writing about?'

Arthur Welling shifted uneasily in his chair.

'She asked me to do her a favour.'

'What favour?'

'To send on something I was looking after for her.'

'What?'

'Some money.'

'Money?' Pickering echoed as if he had never heard of the commodity.

'Yes, she had a biggish win at my club not long before she disappeared and asked me to keep the money personally for her until she needed it.'

'How much?'

'Just over four hundred pounds.'

Sergeant York leant forward and said quietly: 'How could you send her the money if you didn't know her address?'

'Yes, how?' Pickering enquired.

'I had to send it to her care of the Trafalgar Square post office in London.'

'By cheque?'

'No, money order.'

'You're making all this up as you go along, aren't you?' Pickering said after a pause.

'No, it's the truth.'

'How many times has Janet Berry been in touch with you since she left Mongton?'

'I think it's a couple of phone calls and that one letter.'

'She obviously told you what happened in Mr Gray's flat that weekend?'

'No.'

'But surely you asked her?'

'I didn't.'

'You didn't?' Pickering said incredulously. 'You never asked her what had happened to Mr Gray?'

'Or who was the dead person in his bed?' Sergeant York interjected.

'No. And I'll tell you why I didn't,' Arthur Welling said with a sudden show of anger. 'It was because I didn't want to become involved. It was none of my business, and I was determined to stay right out of it. I have enough problems running my clubs properly and I had no wish to add to them.'

'It strikes me you're adding to them by the minute,' Pickering observed. 'On present evidence, I can't see your licences ever being renewed. Don't you agree, Sergeant?'

'I do, sir. Mr Welling has obviously forgotten he'll need our goodwill when he applies for renewal.'

'I've done nothing to justify anyone opposing my licence.'

'Oh, no? Obstructing the police by telling them fairy stories in a murder enquiry? You'll be lucky if you only lose your licence and not your liberty as well.'

'Now you're threatening me.'

'I'm merely pointing out the realities of the situation.'

Arthur Welling glowered at the table between him and his inquisitors. He was certain somebody was trying to set him up and he didn't like the feeling at all. Who on earth had seen him go to Clifftop Rise that evening? It seemed that he must have been followed.

'Shall we start again?' Pickering said after an ominous pause. 'Let me try to help your memory. Presumably you went to Clifftop Rise on Janet Berry's behalf and not on your own initiative, is that right?' When Welling said nothing, he went on: 'Perhaps she asked you to go and make sure she hadn't left a cake baking in the oven, yes?'

'She wanted me to see if the front door had been locked,' he said grimly.

'And had it?'

'Yes.'

'Why was she worried about that?'

'She just was.'

'You never asked her?'

'No.'

'How did you come by a key to let yourself in?'

'She sent it to me.'

'You said just now you'd had only one letter from her, the one that was misdelivered to Mrs Henderson, and that certainly didn't contain a key.'

'I think there'd been an earlier letter.'

'Why should she send you a key to the bungalow?'

'In case she wanted me to go there for something.'

'You knew that Mr Gray had been held there after he'd disappeared from his flat?'

'I quite definitely didn't know that.'

'You're in this up to your neck, aren't you?' Pickering said with quiet menace.

Arthur Welling winced and shifted in his chair.

'Look,' he said with a note of desperation, 'I'll tell you all I know, but you'll have to believe me.'

'There are no "have to's" about it,' Pickering replied.

'I got to know Janet Berry through her becoming a neighbour. I felt sorry for her as she didn't seem to know anybody in the district, and so not long after her arrival at Mr Gray's I invited her to dinner at the Golden Sands Club. There was nothing very special about that; after all, I'd asked Mrs Fox, too, on one occasion. . . .'

'Did you fall in love with her?'

'No. I thought she was quite attractive, but she wasn't my type.'

'You like them younger and blonder, I believe,' Sergeant York put in.

Welling made a sour face. 'Let's just say that Janet Berry held no sexual appeal for me.'

'Or you for her?'

'No. She's still very much in love with her husband—'

'Her husband?' Sergeant York interjected in a voice of total surprise.

'Yes.'

'Where's he been all this time?'

'For most of it, in prison. He was doing two and a half years for fraud.'

'When did he come out?'

'About a month before Mr Gray's disappearance.'

'Was he living at Clifftop Rise?' Sergeant York asked keenly, remembering the list of groceries from Melissa's Foodstore.

'Yes.'

'And did you meet him during that time?' Pickering asked.

'She brought him to the Golden Sands on one occasion.'

'How long had the Berrys owned this derelict bungalow?'

'I can't tell you. But that's why she took a job in Mongton, so

124

that she could keep an eye on the place while her husband was absent.'

'What's his name?'

'I knew him as Geoff.'

'Geoff Berry?'

Welling shrugged. 'I suppose so.'

'The letter you received from Janet Berry was postmarked Birmingham. What were they doing there?'

'Lying low, I imagine.'

'Because they knew the police were looking for them? For her, anyway?'

Welling merely shrugged again.

Chief Inspector Pickering leant forward and flexed his fingers as if about to give a piano recital.

'Why did Mrs Berry abduct Mr Gray?' he asked abruptly.

'I don't believe he was abducted.'

'Are you saying they went off from Southview Court like a honeymoon couple?'

'I wasn't there. I didn't even know they'd gone until Mrs Henderson came back from her weekend away and said she couldn't get any answer. That's the truth.'

'Are you saying that Mrs Berry hadn't already been in touch with you then?'

'She definitely hadn't.'

'When did she first make contact?'

'About a week later.'

'What was that about?'

Arthur Welling shifted in his chair again. 'She wanted to know what was happening. Had the police been around?'

'And you told her they had?'

'Yes.'

'And presumably you asked where she was?'

'No.'

'And where Mr Gray was?'

'No.'

'And who the stranger in his bed was?'

'No.'

'Was that because you already knew the answers to all those questions?'

'No, it's not,' Welling shouted back angrily.

'Whose body was it in Mr Gray's bed?'

'I've no idea. That's the truth.'

'And you never even asked?'

'No, because I didn't want to become involved. The less I knew, the better. I was already regretting. . . .' His voice tailed off.

'Yes? What were you regretting?'

'Ever having taken pity on her.'

'Did she have some hold over you?'

'No.'

'After you'd been to the bungalow to check, as you say, whether the front door was locked, how were you to let her know?'

'She said she'd phone me, but she never has. I'd no way of getting in touch with her.'

'Anything else to ask Mr Welling?' Pickering said, turning to Sergeant York. York leant over and whispered in his superior's ear. Pickering appeared to reflect for a moment before deciding not to follow up the suggestion. 'Have you anything else to tell us, Mr Welling?' Welling shook his head firmly. 'Well, don't think for a moment you're in the clear! Far from it. If you do have any further information, much better to tell us now than have us dig it out later.'

Arthur Welling rose stiffly and, giving Pickering a brief nod, moved towards the door, which Sergeant York held open for him. When York returned to the room a few minutes later, he immediately said: 'I'm still damned sure he recognised the dead man's face from the photo I showed him. I thought you might have pressed him on that, sir.'

'Better to keep something up our sleeves,' Pickering said mildly. 'Timing is all-important in an interrogation.' From his expression, York was unconvinced, and Pickering went on: 'As a matter of fact, if he did recognise the dead man from the photo you showed him and registered surprise, it points to the fact that he hadn't previously known who had been found in the old boy's bed. That, of course, is what he's told us today – possibly one of his few truthful answers.'

CHAPTER 14

JANET BERRY was on edge – not that there was anything new about that during the past two weeks.

She was waiting with impatience for her husband to come home, which added to her restlessness. He had gone to meet the contact who was getting them new passports. They were supposed to have been ready two days before, but there'd been some snag or other. As soon as they had hold of this documentary confirmation of their new identities, they could leave the country. Mr and Mrs Berry would shed their outer skins and slip into those of Mr and Mrs Porter, who would then fly off to a new life abroad.

She stubbed out a cigarette in the overflowing ashtray and went and gazed at her face in the mirror over the mantel-piece. Mr Gray would certainly never have recognised her. Her straight mouse-coloured hair had been transformed so that she was now a frizzy blonde with an aggressive fringe. She had also used make-up to alter her mouth and give her face a harder, more angular look.

From the mirror she went and peered out of the window, hoping to see her husband coming along the road. But there were only a couple of boys kicking a football and laughing uproariously whenever it bounced off a parked car.

It was a terraced street in a run-down area of south London. The house in which they were staying belonged to a relative of her husband, who had rented them her upstairs front room. She was a cranky old girl, and she and Janet had taken an instant dislike to one another. However, she seldom stirred from her kitchen and didn't concern herself with their comings and goings. They had paid her two weeks' rent in advance, which kept her quiet.

Janet wasn't sure that London was any safer than the Midlands. She'd been thoroughly jumpy ever since they'd been spotted in a Birmingham supermarket. That had been the determining factor in her altering her appearance. What a nightmare the whole affair had become! Mr Gray was dead, and she and her husband were on the run. She no longer dared call Arthur Welling as she suspected his telephone might be tapped. As for the bungalow at Beachdean, they were unlikely to see that again. But not even that mattered as long as they could get safely abroad.

She had been badly shaken when she read about Mr Gray's body being washed up on the beach. She had scanned the newspapers each day since, but without learning anything further. It was as if a conspiracy of silence had been formed to keep them in suspense. That was why she had asked Arthur Welling to go and check that Mr Gray's remains were no longer at the bungalow.

She couldn't help wondering what Rosa Epton thought of her now. She hadn't much cared for her, but fortunately they didn't need to see much of one another. The person she had really disliked was Mrs Henderson, whom she regarded as a dangerously bossy and interfering woman. She was never deceived by her parade of so-called virtues.

And the irony of the whole situation was that she was as much in the dark about certain aspects of what had happened as anyone else. The police clearly believed she held the key to the whole mysterious happening, but it wasn't so. Not that she had any hope of persuading them.

Only Mr Gray knew all the whys and wherefores, and he could no longer provide any explanations. Nobody would believe her if she told them she was genuinely sorry he was dead. But in a perverse way it was true.

She heard the front door open, followed by footsteps on the stairs, and she ran across the room to meet her husband. One glance at his face told her the worst.

'You haven't got them?' she said.

'Nope.'

'Why not? What's happened this time?'

'They're just not ready, that's all.'

'But you were promised them today.'

128

'I know.' He sighed. 'Stan says he'll definitely have them next week.'

'By next week we'll probably have been arrested,' she said bitterly.

CHAPTER 15

Rosa felt she ought to phone and find out how Philip Tresant was. Although the case was over, it seemed to be one where a follow-up interest was called for. It was more her sympathy for Jean Tresant that prompted her to take an initiative. She felt desperately sorry for the woman. Admittedly, she had chosen to marry Philip, but Rosa couldn't help wondering if she would have done so had she been able to see what the future held. At least there appeared to be no shortage of money in the family, which was a help in almost every situation. It certainly wasn't a case of Philip having taken five pounds from the offertory in order to buy bread for his children.

Although Rosa had secured his acquittal, she didn't doubt that he would go on being light-fingered. About the only thing that might cure him would be having his hands chopped off, as would happen in some Arab countries. She didn't believe that any amount of psychiatry would reform him. The habit was too ingrained, and it was this that made Rosa fear for his wife and children. Sooner or later they were bound to suffer the public shame a conviction would bring. Perhaps, she reflected, it might have been better if he'd been exposed earlier, if ranks hadn't always closed to protect him from scandal. She didn't know whether case-histories revealed one basic cause for kleptomania or whether they were as numerous as winter viruses. She was sure that sexual motivation would figure somewhere in any psychiatrist's explanation.

With these thoughts running through her head, she asked Stephanie to put through a call and see if anyone was at home.

'Will you speak to either Mr or Mrs Tresant?' Stephanie enquired.

'Yes. I hope she'll answer as I'd sooner speak to her than to him. But, if *he* does, you can't very well say I'll only speak to his wife.'

'Leave it to me,' Stephanie said, as if nothing was beyond her powers. Half a minute later Rosa's phone buzzed and Stephanie announced in a cool detached tone: 'Mrs Tresant on the line, Miss Epton.'

'I thought I'd just call and enquire how your husband is,' Rosa said. 'Has he gone back to work yet?'

'I'm afraid not,' Jean Tresant said in an anxious voice. 'We've had one worry after another. Two days after the case, just when I was hoping to get Philip back on his feet and leading a normal life again, we got a message to say his brother was missing. I think I told you he lived on his own in north London – Muswell Hill to be exact. A neighbour of his phoned to say he hadn't see Malcolm for several days and hoped he was all right. He thought he might be staying with us. Naturally, Philip was terribly worried as his brother doesn't have good health and we'd heard nothing from him for some time. Anyway, Philip's always had a key to Malcolm's flat and so he immediately went up there to see if he could find out what had happened.' She paused. 'At least he didn't find Malcolm lying dead on the floor but, that apart, there was no indication as to where he might be.'

'Did the neighbour say how long he'd been missing?'

'No. He'd been away himself, so he had no idea. They weren't close friends or anything like that. But he knew Malcolm had a brother and he traced us through the telephone directory. When Philip came back from visiting his flat, his nerves were in a terrible state. I said we ought to phone the police, but he wouldn't hear of it. I'm afraid he's rather anti-police as a result of his own experiences. However, I did phone round a number of hospitals. You see, I thought he might have had a stroke and be lying in a hospital bed unable to speak or let anyone know who he was. They were all as helpful as they could be, but none of them had a patient answering Malcolm's description.'

'I'm terribly sorry to hear all this,' Rosa said. 'You really are

131

having more than your share of worry.'

'I know. I keep on wondering what'll happen next.'

'Has Dr Miller been to see Philip?'

'He called in the day after the case, but it was too soon for him to be able to make any assessment. Philip was still in a state of shock.'

'Perhaps worrying about his brother will help him forget his own anxieties,' Rosa said. 'It sometimes works that way.'

'At the moment, I can't see the wood for the trees. I suppose our life will eventually get back to normal, but heaven knows when.'

'Does Philip show any inclination to go back to work?'

There was a sudden heavy silence. Then, in a voice full of pent-up emotion, Jean Tresant said: 'He's resigned from his firm. He doesn't know that I overheard him speaking on the phone and saying he wouldn't be coming back.'

'Shouldn't you tell him you're aware of what he's done?'

'I couldn't, Miss Epton. I just couldn't. I know it's cowardly of me, but I feel I can only cope with one thing at a time. Moreover, it's not the end of the world. We shan't be on the breadline. The most important thing is for him to regain his health. I spoke to Dr Miller today, and he's promised to get Philip into hospital for a complete check-up.'

'Have you told Philip?'

'I had to tell him,' she said in an anguished tone. 'He came into the room while I was talking to the doctor and wanted to know what it was about. I'd much sooner have chosen my own moment to tell him.'

'What was his reaction?'

'He said nothing. He just turned and walked out of the room without a word.' Rosa could tell that Jean Tresant was close to tears as she went on: 'There are times when I feel I'm married to a complete stranger. He's so different from the Philip I once knew.'

'Let's hope Dr Miller can get him into hospital quickly,' Rosa said. 'In the meantime, if there's anything at all I can do, let me know. I know you've got your family and lots of friends, but sometimes it's easier to talk to someone outside one's immediate circle.'

'That's very good of you and I won't forget. I'll certainly

keep you in touch with what happens.'

'I hope you soon have reassuring news about your brother-in-law.'

'Oh, so do I!' She let out a heartfelt sigh. 'At least their parents are not alive to worry about their sons. I'm grateful for that.'

Rosa decided that Jean Tresant was an even nicer woman than she had thought. After putting down the telephone she went along to Robin's room. She had heard him come in and she now ascertained from Stephanie that he wasn't expecting any visitors.

'Are you prepared to be interrupted?' she asked, putting her head round his door.

'Never more so,' he said. 'Anything to put off dictating an awkward brief to counsel.'

'In what way awkward?'

'I want to try to persuade him to take a line he won't like.'

'I thought solicitors were meant to give instructions to counsel,' Rosa observed wryly.

'If I'm too didactic, he might return the brief, and I don't want him to do that. Anyway, start interrupting me....'

'The latest piece of news is that Janet Berry has a husband. He came out of prison about a month before Mr Gray vanished.'

'Where'd you learn that?'

'From Sergeant York. He called me this morning. Apparently they had Arthur Welling in for questioning and he blurted it out.'

'Presumably the food from Melissa's Foodstore was to satisfy Mr Berry's appetite?'

Rosa nodded. 'It also means he was on hand to assist his wife when she and Mr Gray moved out.'

'You make it sound like a moonlight flit.'

'It probably was one.'

Robin frowned. 'What do you envisage happened then?'

'It seems more and more obvious that the man found in his bed must have been known to Mr Gray. Supposing he was somebody out of a murky past....'

'Such as?'

'One of his sons. Remember that snapshot I found showing

133

Mr Gray and a woman and two boys. It was obviously a family group. Given that it was taken in 1960, it would make the boys now aged between thirty and forty. That, according to the pathologist, was the age of the dead man.'

'Which age, thirty or forty?'

'Forty. So it fits.'

'Why should he have told you he never had any children?'

'Come to that, why should he have changed his name from Vinter to Gray?'

'You have a point there. He seems to have been somebody with skeletons in a good many cupboards. Anyway, go on. Somehow his son tracks him down to Southview Court and pays him a visit. What follows?'

'They have a row and the son ends up on the floor dead. The pathologist is of the opinion that the fatal injury was caused by his head striking the edge of an iron fender.'

'I didn't know anyone had iron fenders these days,' Robin observed. 'Certainly not people living in modern apartment blocks.'

'Mr Gray's flat is full of such items. His bed would have accommodated Queen Victoria and all her family. The fender forms part of an artificial fireplace.'

'So his visitor bangs his head and dies. What next?'

'Mr Gray and Mrs Berry have to decide what to do. I would imagine Mrs Berry got in touch with her husband, who hurried to her side. They put the body in Mr Gray's bed and the three of them depart.'

'There are an awful lot of unanswered questions arising from that scenario,' Robin remarked. 'First and foremost, it's hardly the conduct you'd expect of a law-abiding citizen.'

'Who's talking about law-abiding citizens?' Rosa said. 'Mr Gray may outwardly have been one, but what about George Vinter?'

'True, but it still strikes me as an unlikely way for him to behave. As you say, Mr Gray was outwardly living the life of a respectable retired gentleman, so why couldn't he have phoned the police? All he had to tell them was that this unknown person arrived at his flat, became aggressive, and in the course of physically defending himself he gave him a push, which unfortunately caused him to fall and bang his head.'

Rosa gave her senior partner a pitying look. 'That's a piece of special pleading, Robin, and you know it. If he had sent for the police, it was only a matter of time before they found out the dead man was his son.'

'They haven't done so yet,' Robin pointed out.

'No ... well ... he must have had good reasons for not wanting to involve the police.'

'Such as?'

'Because he knew he'd committed homicide. It could be Mrs Berry saw what happened and he knew he couldn't get away with saying it was an accident. In any event a police enquiry was bound to uncover his past.'

'Not necessarily. Provided his fingerprints were not on file, his past need never have emerged.'

'He clearly thought it would,' Rosa said, 'and he knew better than us.'

'All right,' Robin said peaceably, 'what happens next? He and the Berrys take refuge in the bungalow at Beachdean, is that it?'

'Yes ... no ... nothing seems to make very good sense, does it?' Rosa said with a note of despair. 'Unless they were both involved, I don't see why Mrs Berry didn't insist on calling the police.'

'With a husband just out of prison that idea may not have appealed to her. But let's continue. The three of them obviously did hide out at the bungalow, so what happens then?'

'If Mr Gray wasn't a prisoner before, he becomes one. We know he was tied up while he was there. The pathologist found marks indicating that, and Peter and I discovered bits of rope underneath the bed.' She paused. 'I suppose he may have left the flat voluntarily, not wanting to face the police, and that at some later stage the Berrys decided to try to make capital out of the situation by holding him captive.'

'Like all speculation, it's a mixture of hit and miss. It's only later we'll know how much was hit and how much miss.'

'Well, at least there's one thing I can find out straight away. I can call Mr Proctor, the newsagent at Benny Common, and ask him whether the Vinters had two sons of school age when they lived there.'

Five minutes later Rosa was back in Robin's room.

135

'Mr Proctor is quite definite that they had no children at all,' she said bleakly. She shook her head in puzzlement. 'Somebody must know whose body it was in the bed. The police think Arthur Welling recognised him, which would mean that Janet Berry probably knows, too. But why does nobody want to identify him?'

'Because it's in somebody's interest that he should remain unidentified.' Rosa made to go, but Robin went on: 'Your theory takes us nearly to the end, but not quite. Mr Gray died of asphyxiation. Who asphyxiated him and how did he get into the sea?'

'You tell me, Robin.'

'I think only the Berrys could tell us.'

'You believe they killed him?'

'I'd take a lot of persuading that they didn't.'

Rosa let out an exasperated sigh. 'It all comes back to the stranger in the bed. Even if he wasn't Mr Gray's son, he must still have been known to him.' With a note of fresh determination she went on: 'What I need to discover is when George Vinter became Vernon Gray. And, even more important, why?'

CHAPTER 16

Rosa decided to phone Mrs Henderson and invite her out to lunch. In the cause of uncovering the strands of Mr Gray's past she was now prepared to tread paths she had previously avoided, and Mrs Henderson must obviously be regarded as a potential source of information.

She had already written to inform her of her legacy and had received a brief formal acknowledgement. So formal, indeed, that Rosa deduced she had expected considerably more than the £500 she was getting.

Nevertheless, the invitation to lunch was immediately accepted and they arranged to meet the very next day at a hotel on the sea-front where, Mrs Henderson said, they would get sensible English food and be able to talk in a quiet atmosphere.

Rosa caught a mid-morning train, which gave her time to walk from the station. She stood for a while gazing out to sea and breathing in the clean tangy air that London couldn't provide. As she watched a small coastal vessel passing slowly across her line of vision, it suddenly occurred to her that Mr Gray's body must have made similar passage. Beachdean was about four miles east, and the point where he'd been washed up was some fifteen miles to the west. She wondered how far off-shore his body had been at the point where she was standing. She could picture it pitching and tossing as it was carried along by the prevailing current, sometimes on the surface, at other times submerged.

Dismissing this somewhat morbid reflection, she turned and made her way to the hotel, which was further along the front.

Mrs Henderson had already arrived and was sitting on a

chair in the lobby, clutching her handbag on her lap as though daring anyone to snatch it.

'I'm so sorry if I'm a bit late,' Rosa said, perfectly certain that she wasn't.

'That's all right,' Mrs Henderson said with one of her toothy smiles, 'I'm always on time for everything.'

'Would you like a drink in the bar before we eat?'

'A glass of sherry would be quite nice,' Mrs Henderson conceded.

They found a corner table, and Rosa ordered the drinks. While waiting for them to come, she said: 'I thought it would be useful if we had a chat, as there are so many curious aspects to what has happened and you probably knew Mr Gray as well as anyone.'

'Better than anyone,' Mrs Henderson said firmly. 'But may I first ask you who is the main beneficiary under his will?'

'Dr Nagy.'

'Dr Nagy!' Mrs Henderson's tone clearly showed her sense of affront. 'What an extraordinary provision! I'm not saying Dr Nagy isn't a good doctor and didn't look after Mr Gray, but they were never friends or on any sort of social terms. You do surprise me.'

'Mr Gray was an altogether extraordinary man,' Rosa observed. 'Were you aware that he had changed his name?'

'No, he never told me,' Mrs Henderson said with a frown. 'When was that?'

'That's what I don't know. Nor why. Did he ever tell you anything about his past?'

'We used to talk a great deal, of course,' Mrs Henderson said expansively, 'but I must confess that he could be very secretive when he chose to be. I soon learnt that he didn't generally enjoy talking about personal matters. He only once referred to his wife's death from a stroke and that was the first time he'd mentioned having been married. But we used to have long discussions about world events and our own country's affairs. He was a very interesting man.'

'I found his wife's death certificate, together with their marriage certificate and Mr Gray's birth certificate,' Rosa said. 'He kept them in the bank. They were all in the name of Vinter. His real name was George Vinter.'

138

'Vinter, Vinter,' Mrs Henderson murmured. 'I never heard him mention that name. You see, although I got to know him well, we both belonged to a generation that respects other people's ·privacy. We never got on first-name terms, for example.'

Rosa was beginning to realise that she had been over-optimistic about their meeting and that, however much Mrs Henderson might wish to appear to have been Mr Gray's confidante, she knew very little more about him than anyone else.

They finished their drinks and went into the dining room, where Mrs Henderson ordered tomato soup, followed by roast pork. Rosa went for fried whitebait and a ham omelette.

'Did Mr Gray ever mention having any children?' she asked as they awaited the arrival of their first course.

'They never had any. He told me he didn't care for children and was glad they weren't blessed,' Mrs Henderson said primly.

Rosa reached into her bag for the snapshot she'd found at the flat and since taken possession of. She passed it across the table, and Mrs Henderson peered at it closely, then turned it over.

'"Exmouth 1960,"' she murmured. Looking up, she said: 'My husband and I had our honeymoon in Exmouth.'

The idea of Mrs Henderson on a honeymoon anywhere was something that had never occurred to Rosa and 'Oh' was the only comment she felt able to make, followed quickly by 'Don't you agree it looks like a family group?'

'Possibly, but the man's not Mr Gray if that's what you're thinking.'

'What makes you say that?' Rosa asked, shaken by Mrs Henderson's certainty. 'I know the features are not very distinct, but it's his build.'

'It isn't Mr Gray, because the man in this snapshot is wearing suede shoes and Mr Gray never wore suede shoes,' Mrs Henderson remarked with the voice of authority.

Rosa laughed good-humouredly. 'Surely it's possible he did before either of us knew him.'

Mrs Henderson shook her head firmly. 'He told me he'd never worn suede shoes in his life. It wasn't long before the

139

Berry woman arrived, and he was complaining one day about the difficulty of finding a pair of comfortable shoes and I suggested suede as they have more give and he said he couldn't bear them and that he'd never worn them in his life and wasn't going to start now.' She gave Rosa a triumphant look. 'That's how I can tell you it's not Mr Gray in this snapshot.'

'Shoes apart, don't you agree it could be him?' Rosa said.

'His shoes are about the only clear detail.'

Rosa could see there was no point in pursuing the matter. Mrs Henderson had delivered her verdict, and nothing was going to make her change it. Rosa herself still believed it was Mr Gray. There were all sorts of reasons why he might have been wearing a pair of suede shoes that day in Exmouth.

'Are the police any nearer to finding the Berry woman?' Mrs Henderson asked, laying down her soup-spoon and sitting back.

'They've found out that she's married and owns a bungalow at Beachdean,' Rosa said, and went on to give Mrs Henderson an edited account of recent events.

'I wouldn't be surprised to hear she's been in prison herself. As you know, I never trusted her, and my instinct is usually right in these matters. Mind you, I wouldn't trust Mr Welling, either, and I'm not a bit surprised to learn he's involved in this unsavoury business.'

Mrs Henderson proceeded to give her views on her neighbours while Rosa ate her omelette. Eventually the waiter removed their plates and brought the sweet-trolley. Mrs Henderson chose sherry trifle, but Rosa said she would wait for coffee.

Quite suddenly Mrs Henderson, who had appeared preoccupied, put down her spoon and said: 'May I see that snapshot again?' Rosa watched as she screwed up her eyes and peered closely at it. 'The older boy's face is vaguely familiar, but at the moment I've no idea where I've seen it.' It was an admission of defeat that clearly rankled.

'Do you mean you recognise him from twenty years ago?'

'There's some sort of fleeting resemblance to somebody I've met, but I can't place it.' She stared distantly across the room, a small blob of cream stuck perilously to her chin. Then, giving her head a frustrated shake, she started eating again. Meanwhile the blob of cream had become dislodged and fallen on to her purple blouse.

'Perhaps you were in Exmouth in 1960,' Rosa said. 'Maybe this family were staying at the same hotel. Memory can play such capricious tricks.'

'I shan't rest until I can bring it to mind.' She sighed. 'At my age one spends so much time trying to remember names and where one has seen something or other. I recently spent days trying to recall the name of someone who'd been at school with my husband and who later became a bishop.'

Rosa smiled. It took Mrs Henderson to chase a bishop down Memory Lane.

The meal over, Mrs Henderson glanced at her watch and let out an exclamation.

'I must dash,' she said. 'There's an afternoon meeting of our church fellowship group, and without me they won't be able to start. Thank you for lunch. Let's hope the police will soon find the Berrys and tidy everything up.'

With this final brisk observation she was gone, leaving Rosa to assess the value of their meeting. The only positive thing she seemed to have learnt was of Mr Gray's aversion to suede shoes.

CHAPTER 17

JANET BERRY'S SENSE OF RELIEF was unbounded as she went about packing the two suitcases out of which they had lived ever since leaving the bungalow. The very day after her husband had been told that their new passports wouldn't be ready until the following week had come a message via one of his public-house contacts to say they were waiting for collection.

Her elation at the news completely overcame the earlier frustration and feeling of let-down that reliance on her husband's contacts so often engendered.

He had set off at once to pick them up, and she had begun packing so that they could depart that same evening. She had no intention, however, of telling the quarrelsome old woman who owned the house until they were ready to walk out of the front door. Their rent was paid up to the end of the week, so she would have no legitimate cause for complaint.

She was in the process of folding a skirt when there was a knock on the door. She paused in mid-motion and frowned. She knew it couldn't be her husband, and on the rare occasions the old woman came to the door she never bothered to knock. And there was nobody else who knew where they were staying. As this was passing through her mind, there came a second knock.

'Are you there, dear?' the old woman said in a hoarse stage-whisper.

Reassured by the familiar voice, and unalerted by the fact she'd been called 'dear' for the very first time, she went across and opened the door.

The old girl stood there in her grubby flowered pinafore, wisps of grey hair falling across her face.

'There's someone 'ere to see you,' she said with a malicious expression.

'Who? I'm not expecting anybody. Anyway, I'm busy.'

'So I see! Packing, aren't you?' As she spoke she moved aside and was replaced in the doorway by two men who were unmistakably police officers.

'Mrs Janet Berry?' the older man said.

Janet shook her head numbly. 'No, there's some mistake. My name's Eileen Porter.'

'She's Janet Berry all right,' the old woman said in a tone that oozed spite. 'I knew she was a bad lot as soon as they came. Then my neighbour told me about a Janet Berry being wanted by the police about a murder.'

'You bloody bitch,' Janet shouted furiously.

'Best not to make a fuss,' the senior officer said in a nanny-like tone. 'We'll come and have a look around while we wait for your husband.'

Janet stood rooted for a moment, then flung herself on the bed racked by convulsive sobs, born of rage, frustration and bitter disappointment.

'Looks like they were about to do a flit,' the old woman said, peering round the door. 'Lucky I called you when I did. I always did 'ave my suspicions about 'er.'

'Perhaps you'd go and wait downstairs, Mrs Ackerman,' the senior officer said. 'We don't want Mr Berry to be frightened off as soon as he comes in.'

'I'll be in my kitchen,' she said and stumped away.

For several minutes the two officers moved purposefully about the room, opening drawers and cupboards, and exchanging whispered comments while Janet Berry sat huddled on the bed, her face buried in her hands.

It was some forty minutes later all three of them heard the front door open and somebody came running upstairs. A second later the bedroom door was flung open.

'Here's your passport, Mrs Porter,' a jubilant Geoff Berry announced.

He was holding it out, and one of the officers stepped forward. 'I'll have that, sir, if you don't mind.' He flicked over the pages and held it up to the light. 'How much did this cost you?' he asked sardonically.

143

It was as though Geoff Berry was being controlled by a dimmer-switch as he stood there trying to take in the situation.

His wife stared at him bleakly, not trusting herself to speak, and he turned towards the officers.

'Very remiss of us, I'm sure; we've not introduced ourselves,' the older one said. 'I'm Detective Sergeant Telford and this is Detective Constable Goodbody. We understand our colleagues in Mongton are anxious to interview you about the disappearance and subsequent death of one Vernon Gray. It's my duty to caution you – everyone knows the caution these days, don't they? – but you'd probably like to save anything you have to say until you get there.'

As he was to remark to DC Goodbody over a pint of beer that evening, 'Nothing in it for us. Let those keen country boys sort out their own murders.'

By the time she reached Mongton, Janet Berry's mood was one of self-preservation, underlined by defiance. Since their arrest she had been kept apart from her husband without any opportunity of communicating with him.

Detective Chief Inspector Pickering had been eagerly awaiting her arrival and was determined to obtain a confession. Hence she found herself being interviewed within a few minutes of stepping out of the police car. On this occasion, Pickering was accompanied by Detective Sergeant Branch, one of his own CID officers. He felt she should be relatively easy prey, softened up by having been on the run for three weeks and by the damaging evidence already assembled against her.

'Let's start at the beginning, Janet,' he said robustly as he fixed her with a steely look. 'Who was the dead man found in Mr Gray's bed?'

'I knew him as John. That's all I can tell you.'

'You've got to do better than that, if we're not going to fall out. John who?'

'I don't know his surname.'

Chief Inspector Pickering gazed at her as a cat might size up a salmon steak, wondering which was the juicier end.

'Where did you first meet him?'

'At the Golden Sands Club.'

144

'Ah! Who introduced you – Mr Welling?'

'No, he introduced himself.'

'Tell me about it.'

'It was one evening about a week before everything happened. I was there having a quiet drink on my own. . . .'

'What time would this have been?'

'Around nine o'clock. I'd noticed him staring at me from the other side of the room, when suddenly he got up and came across. He asked if he could buy me a drink, and I accepted. When he returned with our drinks he sat down and said he believed I worked for Mr Vernon Gray. There seemed no point in denying it, so I told him I did. He then asked me questions about Mr Gray.'

'What sort of questions?'

'About his routine and how physically fit he was.'

'And you gave him this information?'

'Yes. By then he'd bought me another drink and I was enjoying his company.'

'Did you ask him why he wanted to know about Mr Gray?'

She bit her lip and frowned. 'He'd told me it was because Mr Gray had cheated him out of an inheritance and he wanted to confront him about it.'

'And you believed him?'

'Yes. I couldn't see why he should have made up such a story. Also, I considered Mr Gray quite capable of cheating anybody. He was a miserable old man and thoroughly mean.'

'At what stage did he tell you his name was John?'

'When he brought over the first lot of drinks. He just said, "By the way, my name's John".'

'And you never asked him his surname?'

'No. People meeting in clubs and bars often exchange only first names.'

'Did you ask him where he lived?'

'No.'

'So what did he want you to do?'

'He didn't ask me to do anything – at that time. It was when we met two evenings later that he told me how I could help him.'

'Was that at the Golden Sands again?'

'Yes.'

'You'd agreed to meet a him a second time?'

'Why not? He was a nice man and I was glad to have somebody to talk to.'

And probably saw the chance of making a bit of money on the side, Pickering surmised.

'But you already knew he had it in for your employer?' he went on.

She gave a shrug. 'I should think a lot of people had it in for Mr Gray.'

'What about your sense of loyalty?'

'What about it? I did all I was paid to do. Nitpicking old man that he was, he never complained about my work.'

'All right. Tell me about this second meeting. What did John say on that occasion?'

'He said how he'd like to take Mr Gray by surprise, and I agreed to help him. I usually used to slip out around five o'clock every evening to buy a paper. Anyway, it was agreed that the following Saturday I should leave the front door unlocked when I went out and that while I was away John would enter and confront Mr Gray.'

'You say "confront". What did you think he was going to do?'

'Put the frighteners on him, I suppose.'

'Murder him?'

She gave Chief Inspector Pickering a bold look. 'He never mentioned murder and, if that was his intention, he was remarkably unsuccessful, seeing that he ended up dead himself.'

'Was there any reason for choosing that particular Saturday?'

She pulled a wry face. 'Mrs Henderson was going to be away that weekend.'

'And what did you find when you returned to the flat?'

She was silent while she appeared to assemble her thoughts.

'John was lying dead on the lounge floor, and Mr Gray was huddled in a chair. He said that the man had suddenly appeared in front of him, threatening to kill him. That he had jumped up and in the course of a struggle the man had slipped and fallen backwards, striking his head on the fender.' She paused. 'I suppose fear had enabled Mr Gray to summon what reserves of strength he still possessed. But he was in a terrible state by the time I got back, shivering and

146

trembling as though he had a fever.'

'Did he tell you who John was?'

'No.'

'He gave no indication at all of knowing him?'

'None.'

'Did you tell him you'd met John at the Golden Sands?'

'No.'

'What happened next?'

'I said the police would probably think it was murder, and he begged me not to send for the police. He pleaded with me to help him. I got him to bed and gave him a sedative. Later I phoned my husband, and he came to the flat and it was agreed that the three of us should go to our bungalow at Beachdean which you know about.'

'How much actual agreeing did Mr Gray do?'

'He agreed. Otherwise he wouldn't have come.'

'Who put John's body in the bed?'

'My husband and I.'

'Why?'

'It seemed better than leaving him on the floor.'

'Where was Mr Gray by then?'

'We'd got him into a chair.'

'Did John offer you money to let him into the flat?' When she didn't immediately answer, Pickering added: 'How much?'

'I'm not admitting he did,' she said defiantly.

'Let me tell *you* what followed. After lying low at the bungalow for several days, you decided there was no future in staying there any longer and even less in carting an old man around with you, so you murdered him and threw his body over the cliff-edge. That's what happened, isn't it?'

'No. He was definitely alive when we left.'

'I don't believe you. What's more, a jury won't believe you.'

'It's the truth.'

'Whether or not Mr Gray killed John, it's abundantly clear that you and your husband murdered Mr Gray.'

'Not true.'

'You kept him tied up, didn't you?'

'Part of the time and only for his own safety.'

'Explain.'

'The strain began to tell on him and he became a bit violent

147

at times. We were worried he might harm himself.'

'Did you ever consider getting a doctor for him?'

'I'd taken all his various pills with us, so it was just a question of calming him when he got too worked up.'

'By tying his wrists and ankles.'

'Like I said, we only did it for his own safety.'

'And did you leave him tied up when you left, this sick old man, all alone in your bungalow?'

'This sick old man, as you call him, had the strength to knock down somebody much younger than himself. Don't forget that,' she said angrily. 'Anyway, he was perfectly all right when we left.'

Chief Inspector Pickering let out a sigh. Turning to Sergeant Branch he said: 'I don't know about you, but I reckon I've heard a bigger load of lies these past forty-five minutes than you'd get in a mass perjury trial.'

Sergeant Branch nodded solemnly. 'Wouldn't care to be in her shoes, sir. Can't see a jury taking very kindly to somebody who's behaved as callously as Mrs Berry has. Terrible thing, greed. Talk about selling your soul to the devil for a few pieces of silver. That's what she's done, as I see it, sir. And here she is now, facing a murder charge.' He shook his head sorrowfully, as though weighed down by so much venality.

A silence fell, broken by Chief Inspector Pickering when he said: 'Take Mrs Berry back to her cell, Sergeant. Then let's see how we get on with Mr Berry.'

'I want to see a solicitor,' Janet Berry demanded as she was on her way out of the room, but Chief Inspector Pickering didn't appear to hear.

Sitting in his cell Geoff Berry had had more time than he wanted to brood over recent events. He was angry and thoroughly fed up with all that had happened. Like most other criminals he was self-centred, with inexhaustible supplies of self-pity. When things went wrong he immediately looked for someone to blame for his troubles. In the present instance it was his wife who was the target for his bitterness.

He had barely been released from prison before he found himself caught up in a hare-brain scheme that directly led to their present predicament. The fact that he had enthusiastically co-operated in what she'd proposed was conveniently forgotten. It was all her fault.

Also overlooked was her loyalty to him while he'd been inside. They had been married for five years, half of which he had spent in prison. Admittedly she had been good to him, but he'd never really been cut out for marriage, he now told himself.

The honest truth was that she had become infatuated with him and had made all the running in a whirlwind courtship, in which she did most of the courting. She was three years older than he, and they had met at a pub in Coventry where she was working as a barmaid. For him, her chief attraction had been her readiness to keep him supplied with money.

They had been married in a registry office and a few months later had moved south. With her savings she had bought the bungalow at Beachdean. He hadn't been too keen on the idea, but she had said it would be an investment, as property always increased in value. In the event, they spent very little time there as she moved from job to job, mostly working in clubs and bars. He followed, for where she went the money went.

Then he had met an old associate from one of his previous spells in prison and together they had devised a painless way of separating people from their cash. All was going well, and they were showing a nice little profit, when they succumbed to the desire for bigger and quicker profits. It was a fatal change of tactics and led to Geoff being sentenced to two and a half years' imprisonment and his accomplice to eighteen months. That, in itself, was a cause for considerable resentment as, in Geoff Berry's view, they should have received the same sentence. But the stupid old judge had bumbled on about his previous record and how the public must be protected from his depredations.

Anyway, time passed, as it has to even in prison, and he was duly released and took up residence in the bungalow while he sorted himself out. Meanwhile Janet was working for this wealthy old man a few miles away.

He would never forget the Saturday evening she called and said something had happened and he must come as quickly as possible. He'd arrived to find this body on the floor and the old boy doped up in bed. Janet had lost no time in pointing out how the situation could be turned to their financial advantage. They could squeeze the old man for money under threat of reporting him for murder. Though she hadn't actually been present when the man met his death, it would be easy to say she had come into the room and seen Mr Gray kill him. But they needed a bit of time to set things up, so they had best hide out in the bungalow for a few days.

It had seemed a pretty good idea, and around midnight they had left the flat lugging the old boy with them. What with the shock he'd sustained and the dope Janet had given him, they'd almost had to carry him out to the car.

Before leaving, they'd put the dead man in the bed to make the place a bit tidier.

Thereafter, however, everything had turned sour. The old boy, when not under sedation, was cantankerous and even threatened them with the police. They'd been forced to tie him up in case he should manage to reach the telephone. Clearly nothing was going to persuade him to sign away a few of his thousands to keep them quiet.

It had been a bad idea. What's more, it had been Janet's idea, not his. While this thought was drumming inside his head, Detective Sergeant Branch appeared.

'Come on, you. Chief Inspector wants to have a talk with you.'

Geoff Berry glowered. He was in no mood to talk to anyone; equally, sitting alone in his cell had given him too much time to think. Not that he had any choice but to get up and go.

'You've put yourself in a right old mess, haven't you?' Pickering began in the same robustly cheerful vein he had adopted with Janet Berry.

'I don't know what you mean.'

'Kidnapping. Murder. And that's just for starters. Your wife's told us everything.'

'I don't know what you're on about. I've never murdered anyone in my life.'

'You murdered Vernon Gray at 14 Clifftop Rise sometime between Saturday, 5 October, and the following Saturday.'

'That's a load of crap.'

'Of course, if you're prepared to take the whole blame and tell us that your wife only acted under your duress—'

'That's an even bigger load of crap,' he said furiously.

'Well, then, you'd better tell us your side of things.'

'It was all her idea in the first place. She thought the old boy she worked for would be open to a bit of persuasion.'

'Persuasion?'

'That he'd be glad to pay something for her silence.'

'But he wasn't?'

'You can say that again. He was as hard-headed an old bastard as you'd find in any school of millionaires.'

'Was that why you had to kill him?'

'I don't know anything about his death,' Berry said defiantly.

'But you've as good as confessed to murdering him. You admit abducting him and holding him hostage at the bungalow, so nobody's going to believe that you just walked out and left him there to his own devices.'

'He was still alive when *I* left. That's all I can tell you.'

'You mean, you and your wife didn't leave together?'

Berry's gaze shifted to the floor as he said: 'Yes.'

'Which day did you go?'

'Tuesday, following the Saturday.'

'And where did you make for?'

'London.'

'And when did Janet leave?'

'You'd better ask her that. All I know is that she was there when I left.'

Pickering gave a satisfied nod. It had been easier driving a wedge between them than he'd expected.

'And where did you meet up?'

'In Birmingham on the Friday of the same week.'

'Whereabouts in Birmingham?'

'At an address I had.'

'Whose address?'

'It was the home of a bloke I'd met in the nick. I'd promised to look up his wife. Now you can lay off, because I'm not telling you any more.'

'Who helped Janet throw the body in the sea?'

'Can't help you. I wasn't there.'

151

'But she must have told you what had happened when you met up in Birmingham?'

'Well, she didn't, and I didn't want to know.'

'Do I really look that wet behind the ears?' Pickering said, turning to Sergeant Branch. 'What's he think we are, a couple of bean-sacks?' He swung back and glared angrily at Berry. 'If you want to do yourself a service, quit the fairy stories. Tell me what your wife said about disposing of Mr Gray.'

Berry wriggled uncomfortably. 'She just said that he was dead and that she had managed to roll his body over the cliff-edge opposite the bungalow.' He paused and went on nervously: 'She's as strong as an ox. Don't forget she was used to hauling him around his flat. That's the truth.'

The fact that Berry knew it wasn't and that CI Pickering suspected it wasn't left them more or less in the same position. For the time being, at least.

'Take him back to his cell,' Pickering said. 'And don't let him communicate with his wife.'

Maybe later he would provide them with the opportunity of a whispered exchange and arrange to eavesdrop on what they said.

Meanwhile, a cut-throat defence was emerging and that always suited the prosecution.

CHAPTER 18

OLIVE HENDERSON was not given to flights of fancy. Indeed, she was scornful of those who were. The fact was, however, that she had grown increasingly nervous about being Arthur Welling's neighbour. It was an uneasiness that had begun on the day Janet Berry's misdelivered letter had arrived on her doormat. She was sure that, if looks could have killed, she would have fallen dead there and then. Her feelings were such that she had even sought an ally in Mrs Fox, but her approach had received no encouragement from that quarter.

At night when she was alone in her flat, and particularly in the small hours as she lay awake, her fears often assumed disturbing shapes. She felt that evil had stalked the sixth floor of Southview Court ever since poor old Mr Gray had been abducted and murdered. Moreover, she had become convinced that she was a stand-up target for the vicious criminals who'd been involved in his death.

It was two days after her lunch with Rosa that she had a particularly unsettling nightmare. Arthur Welling had cornered her in the lift and tried to remove her tongue with a dentist's forceps. The dream was so scarifying that when she woke up she was afraid to go back to sleep again even though it was still hours before dawn. In the event, she got up, made a pot of tea and went and sat in her lounge with a blanket round her shoulders.

By the time first light came and she had dressed and had her breakfast, she felt better, though the dream still haunted her. It was like a cloying hothouse scent that permeated everywhere.

Fortunately, the day ahead was a busy one, starting with a nine o'clock visit to her dentist. Thereafter a number of good

153

works were lined up, which would occupy her till early afternoon.

She set off just after eight-thirty and after double-locking her front door stood and listened for a moment. All was silent on the sixth floor. For the first time in her life she actually found herself wishing that Mrs Fox would burst into song. Arthur Welling's door was firmly closed and seemed to have acquired a forbidding look of its own.

She took the lift down to the ground floor and then made her way down the flight of stone steps that led to the cavernous basement garage. It was an echoing, poorly lit area that could seem spooky even on a summer's day. It was only recently, however, that Mrs Henderson had become sensitive to its tomb-like atmosphere.

She reached her Mini and got in. Backing it out into the centre she turned the car so that it faced the exit slope, which had a treacherous right-angle turn halfway up. The Charge of the Light Brigade was a saunter compared with the way Mrs Henderson was wont to tackle the slope with racing engine and slipping clutch.

She had just made the right-angle turn when she let out a sudden sharp exclamation. From nowhere there had come into her mind why the boy's face in the photo Rosa Epton had shown her was familiar. At the same moment she was aware of a car rushing down the slope towards her. There was a screech of brakes as the other car stopped dead. Unfortunately, Mrs Henderson's didn't do likewise and there followed a nasty crunch of metal. The impact sent her car bouncing back into a brick wall.

'Are you all right?' Arthur Welling enquired anxiously, speaking through her half-open window.

She tried to focus her gaze, but her head kept lolling to one side.

'You were driving too fast,' she said in a muzzy tone.

'You stupid old cow,' he muttered under his breath in a tone of suppressed fury. Aloud he said: 'Wait here while I go for help.'

In fact, she had no choice but to stay where she was as the doors of her car had jammed and it took the fire brigade to release her. By that time the police and an ambulance had

154

also arrived, while a small crowd of interested spectators stood exchanging comments at the top of the slope.

The doctor who examined her told her she was lucky to have escaped with only minor injuries, but insisted she remain in hospital at least for twenty-four hours.

'But I have a number of important meetings to attend,' she said groggily.

'They can manage without you,' he replied. 'Nobody's indispensable.'

It was not a view Mrs Henderson was disposed to share where her own activities were concerned.

Later as she lay gently fingering her multiple bruises, she had a sudden repeat performance of the flash of recollection that had been responsible in part for her accident.

'I have to phone Miss Epton,' she called out to a passing nurse.

'Later, dear,' the nurse said, pausing to smooth her top sheet and plump up her pillow.

'But it's most urgent.'

'Just lie quietly and rest, dear.'

'But I have to make an important phone call.'

'Nothing's more important than getting you fit again. You've been in a serious accident, and the body takes time to recover when we're not as young as we used to be.'

Mrs Henderson gave up, and the nurse moved away. Worried, however, lest she might suffer selective amnesia as a result of the bang to her head, she reached out for the old-fashioned school slate which rested on top of her bedside locker. A piece of chalk was attached to it by a length of frayed string.

With a shaky hand she wrote herself a memo which would serve as a reminder. It read: 'Boy in snapshot = body in bed.'

Exhausted by the effort, she lay back and closed her eyes. She suddenly felt very tired. The next time the nurse passed the end of her bed she was glad to see that Mrs Henderson had fallen asleep. An hour later, however, something caused her to take a closer look at the patient. It was then clear that Mrs Henderson had passed from sleep into death, having, it transpired, quietly succumbed to a heart attack.

Quickly the nurse drew the curtains around the bed and

arranged for the removal of the body to the hospital mortuary with as little disturbance as possible to other patients in the ward.

She noticed that something had been written on the slate and was about to rub it clean when she had second thoughts and took it instead to her office.

When Sergeant York, unaware of Mrs Henderson's death, arrived that evening to interview her about her accident (he had been specially sent in view of his previous dealings with the sixth-floor residents of Southview Court) the nurse showed him the slate.

'The patient apparently wrote this shortly before she died,' she said. 'It's probably not important, but I thought I'd show it you as she kept on about wanting to make a phone call to a Miss Epton and I wondered if the two things were connected.'

CHAPTER 19

WITH A CHEESE SOUFFLÉ about to be taken out of the oven, the
telephone could not have rung at a more inopportune
moment. Rosa hesitated, wondering whether to ignore the
phone and go ahead with her supper. Whoever was calling
would simply assume she was out and would ring again later –
or not, as the case might be. On the other hand, to answer the
phone would almost certainly mean returning to a travesty of
what a soufflé should be. In the event she lowered the heat of
the oven, crossed her fingers and went off to see who it was.
After all this, it would probably turn out to be a wrong
number.

'Miss Epton?' Sergeant York said in a now well-familiar
voice. 'Sorry to disturb you at home, but I thought you should
know that Mrs Henderson's dead. She died in hospital this
afternoon.'

'What happened?' Rosa asked, half-dreading what she
might be told.

'She was involved in a car accident this morning. She and
Mr Welling had a head-on crash on the slope leading out of
the underground garage at Southview Court. To be fair to
Mr Welling, it seems to have been her fault. Anyway, she was
taken off to hospital with what appeared to be only minor cuts
and bruises and died a few hours later of a heart attack.'
Sergeant York paused before adding: 'It appears to be a
genuine case of death from natural causes.'

'That's all rather sad,' Rosa said. 'But I'm sure she's already
on some celestial committee. Incidentally, she's not my client,
if you were thinking that.'

'No, we know who her solicitor is. He's local and we've
already been in touch with him. The reason I'm calling is

because she told one of the nurses that she had to speak to you urgently. Nurses have a lot of practice at sidestepping patients' demands, and Mrs Henderson was given some soothing reply. However, the nurse later discovered that she had scribbled something on a slate and, putting two and two together, thought it might be connected with her wish to speak to you.'

'What was on the slate?'

'I have it written down here. It said: "Boy in snapshot equals body in bed." Does that make any sense to you?'

'Yes, it does,' Rosa said. 'I'd better explain.'

When she had finished, Sergeant York said: 'I'd like to see the snapshot.'

'Certainly. I'm still inclined to think that, suede shoes or no suede shoes, it's Mr Gray and his wife, except I suppose they were Mr and Mrs Vinter at that time. If the two boys are not their sons, maybe they're the sons of friends. It's a pity the faces are so indistinct. The two adults are wearing hats with brims, and the boys have screwed-up expressions because they're looking straight into the sun.'

'Supposing Mrs Henderson is correct and the older boy is the person we found in Mr Gray's bed. Does that help us identify him? Not really,' he went on, answering his own question. He then told Rosa what Janet Berry had said about the dead man.

Rosa was thoughtful, her cheese soufflé forgotten. 'He's obviously somebody out of Mr Gray's past, and we'd guessed that already.'

'It'll be interesting to show the photograph to Janet Berry and see what she has to say. She may be able to confirm Mrs Henderson's view that the boy and the man she met and knew as John are the same person. I'd like to send somebody up to your office tomorrow morning to collect the snapshot. Would that be convenient?'

'Yes, I'll leave it in an envelope addressed to you with Stephanie, our receptionist.'

After talking for a further few minutes, their conversation ended and Rosa returned to the kitchen which was filled with a strong smell of cheese and scorched paper. She opened the oven door and took out her soufflé, which resembled a recently active volcano. She decided to eat the congealed centre and throw away the rest. A glass of white wine would probably help it down.

As she ate, she found Mrs Henderson occupying her thoughts. Though there were times when she was more of a trial than a help, Rosa knew that, in a perverse way, she was going to miss her.

And, if she was right, who were the figures in that snapshot taken at Exmouth twenty-five years ago?

It was curious that Mrs Henderson had found the older boy's features familiar, whereas she, Rosa, had had some distant chord touched by the younger one's face. She had connected it with a likeness to the man in the photo whom she took to be Mr Gray. But if Mr Gray had never had a son. . . .

CHAPTER 20

POLICE CONSTABLE HACKFORTH was surreptitiously doing his football pools when he became aware of someone awaiting his attention.

'What can I do for you?' he asked, glancing up guiltily.

'My name's William Ashford,' the person said. 'I understand you have an unidentified dead body on your hands and I am wondering if it could be my cousin, Martin Ashford. He disappeared about three weeks ago and hasn't been seen since.'

The man had spoken with a slightly ingratiating air, and PC Hackforth studied him with suspicion, as if he might be laying bogus claim to a valuable reward.

'Where d'you live, Mr Ashwood?' he asked.

'Ashford,' the man corrected him. 'My permanent address is a box number in Kuwait, which is where I work. I happen to be back in England on short leave and went to look up my cousin, only to discover that he had disappeared. Nobody could tell me very much, and I felt I owed it to him to make enquiries. We were both only children and our parents are dead, so that we're a bit short on relatives.'

'Where did your cousin live?'

'In London.'

'It's a sizeable town. Whereabouts?' If PC Hackforth hoped his scepticism would deflate his visitor, he was disappointed.

'He had a flat at 32 Fineleigh Road in Acton, which is on the west side of London.'

'I know where Acton is,' Hackforth said a trifle testily, cross at having been taken for an apparent country bumpkin. 'Anyway, what makes you think his body may be lying unclaimed in our mortuary?'

'I remembered that he used to come down here for the day quite often and I thought it was possible he'd been involved in a fatal accident and nobody had been able to find out who he was. He was always a bit of an eccentric, my cousin. He often used to go off and nobody would know where he was. And then he'd suddenly turn up again.'

'So what are you after, Mr Ashford, apart from finding out if he's our refrigerated guest?'

'I'd like to arrange for a proper burial before I go back to Kuwait.'

'When's that?'

'At the end of next week.'

'And if we don't have his body?'

Ashford gave a small helpless shrug. 'I'll spend the remainder of my leave searching elsewhere.'

'I've heard of some pretty rum holidays in my time,' PC Hackforth remarked, 'but yours is as morbid as any.'

'I haven't got anything else to do and I feel I owe it to my cousin.'

PC Hackforth scratched the back of his head. 'What makes you so sure he's dead? He may just have taken off and be enjoying himself somewhere. After all, you've said he was eccentric.'

'He's never before been away for so long. That's why I'm afraid something's happened to him.' He paused. 'I know I may be on a wild-goose chase, but surely there's no harm in letting me see the body you have.'

'I haven't actually said we did have any unclaimed bodies,' PC Hackforth remarked quickly. 'You'd better take a seat over there and I'll go and make a few enquiries.'

He knew that Sergeant York was somewhere in the building and went in search of him, eventually running him to ground in the canteen. He sat himself down at the table where York was having a cup of tea and a poached egg.

'I've got a real wimp in the front office,' he said and went on to relate what had happened.

'Does he strike you as genuine?' York asked at the end.

'Yes and no.'

'That's very helpful.'

'Come and have a word with him yourself, Sarge. I mean, it

could be that body of yours he's looking for. The one you found in old Gray's bed. The times all fit.'

Sergeant York was thoughtful. It did, indeed, seem a strange quest for anyone to be pursuing. So strange as to arouse instant suspicion.

'Right, I'll come and speak to him as soon as I've finished my meal. Give me three minutes.'

'Shall I give him your name?'

'Give him nothing.'

When, however, Sergeant York reached the reception area a few minutes later, he was met by a dismayed PC Hackforth.

'He's gone, Sarge. He wasn't here when I got back. He must have walked off.'

'Did anyone see him leave.'

'No. WPC Bailey was in the inner office with the door open, but she didn't hear a thing.'

The fact that the man had vanished as abruptly as he'd appeared was proof either that he was a hoaxer or that he had some interest in events at Southview Court, but had been frightened off by PC Hackforth's manner. As it was an unlikely sort of hoax, the second alternative was the more probable.

Sergeant York ran to the entrance and looked up and down the street, but there was nobody in sight who answered William Ashford's description. He returned inside and glared at a worried-looking PC Hackforth.

'Don't blame me, Sarge. It's not my fault he scarpered.'

'I want a full written description of the man, together with all the details he gave you.'

'Yes, Sarge.'

'Within the next half-hour.'

'Will do,' Hackforth replied glumly, saying goodbye to his own refreshment break.

The more he reflected on it, the more Sergeant York became convinced that William Ashford, whoever he was, had, for his own reasons, wished to view the body of the man found in Mr Gray's bed. A body which couldn't be buried until it had been identified.

CHAPTER 21

On the morning following her phone call from Sergeant York, Rosa went straight to court and didn't get into the office until mid-afternoon, when she was surprised to find Ben deputising for Stephanie.

'Hello, Miss Epton,' he said with his customary cheerfulness. 'Steph's had to go home. Her sister's little boy had an accident at school and, as her sister's in hospital having another baby, Steph's gone to sort things out.'

'I hope her nephew isn't badly hurt.'

'He fell over in the playground and gashed his leg. He's got to have a few stitches.'

Whenever Ben stood in for Stephanie, his relish for the job was always apparent. It still surprised Rosa how competently he managed their small switchboard, and there was no doubt that he had effective ways of dealing with importunate callers of whom there were invariably a few.

'By the way,' he said as Rosa moved away towards her office, 'Steph's left a telephone message on your desk. Told me to tell you in case it got buried.'

Rosa had barely reached her room and closed the door when the phone buzzed.

'Mrs Tresant's on the line. Shall I put her through?' Ben asked.

Rosa sighed. 'Yes, I'll take the call,' she said, casting a quick eye at the message Stephanie had typed out and left for her.

'Miss Epton. It's Jean Tresant. I wanted to let you know that things seem better. At least, I hope I'm not deluding myself,' she added with a nervous laugh. 'Philip's been job-hunting, which is the best sign. In fact, he's gone today to see a firm of quantity surveyors who want an office manager.'

'That's splendid news,' Rosa said, without great conviction. 'Did he have his medical check-up?'

'No, it's next week. But Dr Miller has put him on different tablets, which seem to have helped.'

'Where's the job he's hoping to get?'

'In Canterbury.'

'So you'd have to move?'

'Yes, but that's become inevitable anyway after what's happened. It'll be best to make a complete break. Philip's case has caused too many rifts, which will never heal. It doesn't really matter where we go as long as we all remain together. I know I was against a move at first, but I now realise I was wrong. Anyway, I'm sure we shall see you before we leave.'

Rosa took a deep breath. 'As a matter of fact I'll be down your way this evening. May I drop in for a few minutes if that's convenient?'

'That'll be lovely. About what time?'

'Six o'clock.'

'With luck Philip will be back by then and you'll see him, too.'

The conversation ended, Rosa sat back and began to marshal her thoughts. She wished Robin was in, but he never was when she most needed him.

It was several minutes before six when she drew up outside the Tresants' house, but she didn't think that arriving early would matter on this occasion. There were lights on down-stairs, and she wondered if Philip had returned.

Jean Tresant answered the door promptly with a welcom-ing smile. For once it was she who seemed relaxed and Rosa who was tense and suddenly ill-at-ease.

'I'm afraid Philip's not back,' she said as Rosa followed her into their lounge. 'Actually, he phoned soon after I spoke to you and said he was going to stop a further night in Canterbury and do some house-hunting.'

'Does that mean he's got the job he was after?'

'He doesn't yet know, but he likes the area and thinks we might move there anyway. I can't tell you what a relief it is to have him living positively again. Even if he still has bouts of black depression, he shows improvement every day.'

Rosa reflected on the truism that people could usually see

164

what they wanted to see. However, the very fact that Philip was out of the house was, she supposed, a sign of some improvement.

'Has he had any news of his brother?' she asked.

Jean Tresant shook her head forlornly. 'Not a word. Malcolm has vanished as completely as Lord Lucan did. I think Philip has come to terms with the possibility that he'll never see him again. It wasn't that they used to meet very often, and when they did they never seemed to have a great deal in common, but there was always a strong familial bond between them. Philip no longer talks about his brother's disappearance, but I know it's caused him great anguish.' She let out a heavy sigh. 'It's always the uncertainties in life that nag one, don't you find? Not knowing is infinitely worse than actually hearing the worst. Once you know that, your mind starts making adjustments, but being kept in suspense is totally undermining. At least, that's my experience.'

Rosa thought it was most people's, but it didn't help her at this particular moment.

In a somewhat awkward tone she said: 'Do you by any chance have a photograph of Philip's brother?' She expected Jean Tresant to ask her why, but she never did.

'Yes, I'll get out the family album,' she said, going across to a small oak chest and opening it. She brought the album over to the sofa and sat down beside Rosa. She flicked over the pages before depositing it on Rosa's lap. 'That's Malcolm when he was a good deal younger. It must have been taken about ten years ago before their parents died. He doesn't have as much hair now and his face is thinner.'

'Are these all family photos?' Rosa asked, turning the pages.

'Yes. I think I told you previously that I never knew my in-laws. They died within a year of one another. Philip's father committed suicide, and his mother died of a broken heart ten months later. They were a devoted couple.' She gave Rosa a sad little smile. 'You could say I caught Philip in the aftermath of the tragedy when he was looking for stability.'

'I seem to remember your telling me that Philip didn't like talking about what had happened.'

165

'That's right. It's a closed chapter of his life. The subject's always been taboo.'

'Most families have tragedies of one sort or another in their backgrounds,' Rosa said sombrely.

Shortly afterwards she took her leave of Jean Tresant and drove home, her mind in a turmoil.

She now knew why the younger boy's face in the snapshot she had found at Mr Gray's flat had seemed distantly familiar, for she had seen its duplicate in the Tresant album. It had been the Tresant family on holiday in Exmouth. Philip was the smaller boy and it was his father who was wearing the suede shoes and panama hat. She had jumped to a hastily false conclusion in persuading herself that the man must be Mr Gray.

And Mrs Henderson had been right, too, in her recognition of the older son as the person found in Mr Gray's bed. Sooner or later Jean Tresant would have to find out where her brother-in-law had been all this time.

Everything had begun to fall into place when she read the message Stephanie had left on her desk.

It ran: 'Miss Dove of Caring Removals phoned. She says that the owner of J. T. Furniture of Brackingham was a Mr James Tresant. After the business went bankrupt with huge debts, Mr T. shot himself. She could probably find out further details if you want.'

Rosa thought that she could now guess them.

CHAPTER 22

'ARE YOU ALL RIGHT, MATE?' the young man who was fishing asked.

The man to whom he spoke gave a slight nod, but didn't bother to turn his head and see who was addressing him.

'Quite sure?'

This time the man murmured something which the other took to be assent, so that he returned to where he had left his rod and line. He was one of those fanatical fishermen who spent most of his free time fishing off the pier in all weathers.

Fishing was one thing on a bitingly cold November day, whereas leaning on a rail and staring out to sea was far less explicable. Certainly when it went on for over thirty minutes.

Three-quarters of an hour later the young man was ready to pack up and go home. It wasn't the cold but the absence of fish that dictated his decision.

The other man was still in the same position, and the fisherman approached him again.

'I'm off home,' he said in a conversational tone. 'You must be bloody cold, too. Come and have a cup of tea.'

The older man gave a slight shake of the head, but still didn't look round. For a moment the young man stood in indecision, then shouldering his gear he moved slowly away. He glanced back several times, but the tableau remained unchanged. He didn't like leaving the other man alone at the end of the pier in the gathering gloom of a November afternoon. On the other hand, it was a free country and he had at least held out a Christian hand. He told himself that, if the man intended to commit suicide, he would surely have done so without such lengthy contemplation of the deed. The longer people delayed the final step, the less likely they were to take it. This, at least, was the popular belief, but he knew it to be a myth. It had been contradicted a number of times during his relatively short length of police service. By the time he reached the end of the pier, he had decided to phone the station and pass his anxieties on to a colleague on duty.

Thus it was that half an hour later Sergeant York hurried along the pier, propelled more by hope than by expectation. As he rounded the shuttered cafeteria at the end he strained his eyes for sight of the man PC Yates had phoned in about. But there was no longer anyone standing against the rail.

Either the man had jumped, or he had left the pier on Yates's heels.

Then he saw what appeared to be a pair of legs sticking out from one of the seat shelters. He hastened forward and found a man huddled in a corner, his coat collar turned up so that his head was almost hidden. York gave his arm a brisk shake.

'Mr Ashford?' he said.

The man gave him a dazed look, but said nothing.

'Or should I say Mr Tresant?'

CHAPTER 23

IT WAS THE NEXT DAY that Rosa received another call from Sergeant York which left her feeling confused and depressed. She had spoken to Robin on the telephone when she got back from her visit to Jean Tresant and she now went along to his room.

He could tell from her face that she needed to talk, so pushing away the file he had been reading he said: 'Have a chair and give me today's bulletin.'

'Philip Tresant has been charged with Mr Gray's murder,' she replied bleakly. 'Or George Vinter's murder, to be more precise. Not that names matter very much when you're dead.'

'Where was Tresant arrested?'

'At the end of Mongton pier. An off-duty police officer, who was fishing, saw him and thought he looked like a potential suicide, so when he left to go home he phoned the station and reported the fact. The description he gave matched that of a man calling himself William Ashford who'd visited the police station the previous day wanting to see their unidentified body, which he believed might be his missing cousin. He'd spun a story about being on leave from the Middle East and finding his cousin had vanished. Anyway, when the officer to whom he had told this went off to find Sergeant York, Mr Ashford did his own disappearing trick. Yesterday afternoon, when the PC who'd been fishing on the pier phoned in, Sergeant York happened to be around and decided there was an outside chance it was their visitor of the previous day.' Rosa let out a heavy sigh. 'It seems Philip Tresant had been on the pier over three hours wrestling with the decision whether to throw himself off. Sergeant York says he was in a state of mental exhaustion and made no attempt to deny his identity.'

'What about the job in Canterbury he was said to have been after?' Robin asked.

'I suspect he never went anywhere near Canterbury. He told his wife that simply to keep her happy. Apparently he'd become obsessed with giving his brother a Christian burial. That's why he made a not very subtle or thought-out attempt to claim the body.'

'How did he know his brother's body was in Mongton mortuary?'

'He's told the police everything,' Rosa said. 'According to Sergeant York, he was obviously relieved to get it off his chest.'

'The police always like to be able to say that,' Robin observed drily. 'Though it is quite often true. But you haven't answered my question.'

Rosa took a deep breath. 'What he's told the police is that his father owned and ran a small but highly successful furniture factory in Brackingham and that George Vinter was his trusted employee for over thirty years. Starting as a clerk and ending up as the company secretary and accountant. He became a friend of the family, and Philip and his brother always called him Uncle George. Then, one fine spring morning about eight or nine years ago, Uncle George failed to turn up for work and slowly the awful truth emerged. For years he had been syphoning off the company's profits and covering his defalcations by fraudulent entries in the books. It was reckoned he had got away with just under two hundred thousand pounds. Obviously the 1978 bank statement in the name of William Corley that I found at the flat related to money he had salted away. As a result the business was bankrupted and James Tresant found himself unable to meet his various liabilities. After a year of struggle, he felt he could no longer face the future and he shot himself. His wife, who was devoted to him, never got over the shock and died about ten months later.'

'How old were the boys when this all happened?'

'Malcolm was about thirty and Philip twenty-three.'

'And Mr Vinter had meanwhile disappeared?'

'Completely, without any trace. He'd had time, of course, to cover his tracks in advance and prepare a false identity.'

170

'I suppose the two sons saw him not only as a swindler, but also as being responsible for the death of their parents?'

'They regarded him as a double murderer and they determined they would go to the ends of the earth to bring him to justice, however long it might take.'

'Their own justice?'

Rosa shrugged. 'I don't know what their original intention was, but that's how it has turned out. It seems that Malcolm Tresant spent his time following up leads, until eventually he got on to Mr Gray, who by then was living comfortably at Southview Court. He and Philip then set their plan. Malcolm, as we know from the post-mortem examination, had a heart condition and didn't expect to live more than five or six years. And he was perfectly prepared, if necessary, to spend them in prison, content in the knowledge that he had avenged his parents' memory. We know from Janet Berry, however, what actually happened, which left Philip with a further death to avenge. He found out what had happened when Malcolm never returned. His brother had told him about meeting Janet Berry, whom he had obviously had under surveillance, and about her bungalow at Beachdean. Anyway, Philip decided to start his own investigation there. He probably didn't have any fixed plan in his head or even know what he'd discover when he got there. What he did find was a weak, frail Mr Gray trussed up on a bed where the Berrys had left him when they cleared off a day or so earlier.' Rosa shook her head sadly. 'He smothered him with a cushion and, when it was dark, lugged the body to the cliff-edge and toppled it over.'

Robin was thoughtful for a moment. 'I take it that it wasn't just a coincidence that Philip Tresant came knocking at our door?'

'I imagine Malcolm found out from Janet Berry that I was Mr Gray's lawyer, so that when Philip needed the services of a solicitor in connection with the theft charge Malcolm suggested he come to me. I think I've mentioned how I used to catch him trying to read things on my desk. Malcolm probably asked him to find out anything he could about my dealings with Mr Gray. If he couldn't, it didn't really matter as he still needed a lawyer.'

'I would think', Robin said in a reflective voice, 'that he'll have a good defence of diminished responsibility, given his obviously unstable character. It would take an extremely hard-hearted jury to convict him of murder.'

'It would have been better for everyone if he *had* jumped off the pier,' Rosa said.

'I'm sure Sergeant York wouldn't agree with you. The police never like to be deprived of their prey.'

'Sergeant York's a good officer and I'm glad that, if anyone had to arrest Philip Tresant, it was he. He'd done a lot of work on the case and then had to turn it over to the CID.'

'I hope he's duly grateful for all the help you gave him.'

'It was a two-way traffic,' Rosa said. She gave Robin a wan smile. 'He wanted to know if I'd be defending Philip on the murder charge, and I told him no.'

'I agree you couldn't very well do that. Incidentally, I wonder if we'll make the record book by having one of our clients murder another?'

'More likely to get us into the Black Museum,' Rosa observed.

'Did Sergeant York say what was going to happen to the Berrys?'

'I understand they've already got their lawyers scratching around for a charge. The common-law offence of kidnapping seems the favourite at the moment, but there may be evidential difficulties without the victim being able to testify.'

'I bet they'll rake up something.'

Rosa let out a heavy sigh. 'How on earth do I begin to wind up Mr Gray's estate? It's tainted money.'

'You'd best wait until all the criminal charges have been disposed of. Is there anyone who might contest the will?'

'I've no idea.'

'In the meantime you can take counsel's opinion on the whole messy affair. The estate can afford the best advice you can get.'

'I feel so desperately sorry for Jean Tresant,' Rosa said in an anguished voice. 'What that poor woman has gone through, with even worse to come.'

Robin gave a sympathetic nod.

'Give it a day or two and then go and see her.'

172

His phone buzzed, and he lifted the receiver.

'It's for you,' he said, passing it to Rosa.

'You remember that television programme you appeared on?' Stephanie said in a deadpan voice. 'I've got the producer's secretary on the line. They'd like you to be on it again.'

'Tell them in the nicest possible way that I'm still coping with problems arising from my last appearance – and shall be for the foreseeable future.'

'I'll say that, like Miss Otis, Miss Epton regrets,' Stephanie observed drily.

Rosa laughed. 'Better still, Steph, sing it.'